The Widow of The Valley

EMMA HARDWICK

Drina
ROMANCE
PUBLISHING

COPYRIGHT

Title: The Widow of the Valley

First published in 2020

Copyright © 2020 Emma Hardwick

ISBN: 9798476239888 (Paperback)

BOOK CARD

Other books by Emma Hardwick

The Urchin of Walton Hall

Forging the Shilling Girl

The Sailor's Lost Daughters

The Scullery Maid's Salvation

The Widow of the Valley

The Christmas Songbird

The Slum Lady

The Vicar's Wife

The Lost Girl's Beacon of Hope

The Slum Sisters' Wish

Finley's Christmas Secret

CONTENTS

1

THE TRIP TO SUNDAY SCHOOL

Derryn Evans buttoned her daughter's coat up to her chin, wrapped a woolly scarf around her neck, then pulled down her bonnet firmly, hoping it would stay in place.

"But I am not cold, Ma!" the tiny girl grizzled impatiently, squirming as she tried to take everything off again. "Are you listening to me, Ma?"

"A little less chit-chat, my girl, if you please. We need to get a move on, Becca," the mother protested in vain as she smiled down at her beloved child.

Becca didn't return the smile. Her serious little face frowned and her mouth puckered up, poised to ask another question.

"I'm not going anywhere Ma until you tell me—when will I go to a proper school?"

"We'll have to discuss that with Miss Bevan," answered Derryn. "You've only just turned five. I am sure Miss will call for you soon."

"I want to read everything!" the girl said with determination. "Miss Bevan has shelves and shelves full of books, Ma. She says we can take them home to read. She calls it a la—? Um, lie—?"

"Library?" volunteered Derryn gently.

"Yes, it's called a library." the girl agreed with confidence, keen to pretend she hadn't forgotten the term. "Come on, Ma," Becca ordered. "I don't mean to be rude, but I cannot be late for Sunday school—come— on!"

Derryn shook her head in amusement.

"And who is rushing now?" her mother asked, trying not to laugh.

Derryn took Becca's hand, and they stepped from their tiny home into a narrow lane between the miners' cottages. The church bells rang out their first reminder of the day. It had rained the night before. They had to fight their way through an ankle-deep mixture of coal dust, mud and clinker. It was only half-past nine, but the skies were a low and deep grey. Foreboding.

The chimneys of the village and the coal mine had been belching black billowing smoke into the air all night, so thick and acrid it often prevented any sunlight reaching the ground even if the sky cleared.

Derryn and Becca walked up toward the small village making their way towards the High Street. Once there, they began the long leg of the walk. It would lead them up the hill to the sturdy stone church that overlooked the village and colliery. The wind growled as it forced its way off the hillside and down between the shops. It made their bonnet brims flutter and their fastenings flap like whips.

As they approached their destination, they could see the candles were already lit inside the building. The stained-glass windows twinkled with jewel-like colours making it look welcoming in the winter gloom.

St. Martins sat upon the hill as if keeping vigil over the small community, the village that nestled in the valley below. It was a picture-postcard place with tiny shops, quaint cottages, and the red-bricked schoolhouse.

A little lower were more houses comprised mostly of rows of miners' cottages which neighboured the colliery and grimy misery. In the dark of the morning, the entire colliery was almost invisible. That glimmer was extinguished as the rain returned, mercilessly stinging their faces. Derryn rushed Becca through the churchyard towards the shelter to be found behind the sturdy oak entrance doors.

On a sunny day, everybody would be standing about chatting, but today they had all gathered at the back of the nave. As the mother and daughter crept inside, they were greeted by a crunch of bodies and voices. At the same time, the other children darted amongst the adults' forest of legs calling out for their friends.

"Morning, Derryn," greeted Derryn's closest friend, Bronwyn with a warm smile. "What do you reckon to this weather then? I've been wondering how long you were going to take to get here in this gale," she chuckled.

"I was up early. I had to prepare Tiny's lunch. He is keen as mustard to take on those extra shifts. I almost didn't come here today. My bed was calling to me. Becca was insistent mind. As always she spent her time nagging me to leave and then slowing us down with her endless questions."

Derryn was fighting to remove Becca's wet coat and bonnet. Finally, the girl conceded and stood still.

"Aye, I know the feeling, my love, I could have slept in too. Not much chance of that, though!" laughed Bronwyn. "What time did Tiny go in then?"

"His shift started at six, but I was up earlier to get him ready."

"Bleedin' men can't even pack a lunch for themselves and give ya a day's rest once a week. Ideas above their station, some of them," complained Bronwyn.

"Bronnie! What's with the cursing' in the church? Pack it in before Reverend Hughes hears you." whispered Derryn trying her best not to break into giggles.

Becca tugged at her mother's skirt.

"What now, child?" asked Derryn.

Becca was impatient to leave her mother and was bouncing from one foot to the other.

"Ma, can I go now?" she nagged.

"Oh, yes, my angel, you go." Derryn told the little girl, "I'll see you later."

Derryn watched the child run toward the makeshift classroom at the back of the chapel. She was overwhelmed with love as she watched Becca's little blonde head bobbing about until she was swallowed by the crowd of unruly children waiting for Miss Bevan.

The tiny church was at full capacity for nobody could ever say that the weather kept the Welsh away from the church, despite their gossipy protestations when they struggled with it.

The choir congregated before the alter in their pure white cassocks and deep red surplices. Derryn would have been one of them, had she been able to go to practice that week. The choir was a proud product of their nation. God had given them the talent to sing, and they had perfected it by practising.

The service opened with the great hymn Amazing Grace, and the voices of the small mining community rose upon the air in powerful unison. The deep tenors and baritones harmonised with the altos, while the sopranos escalated the beautiful sound into a heavenly chorus. The music exalted the congregation high above the misery of the wintery weather and the clinging grey smog.

Somewhere during the lines 'Through many dangers, toils and snares we have already come', their well-trained ears picked up a disharmony in the chords. The choir and congregation ignored it, singing louder in an attempt to drown the faults and correct the tune. But the shrill discord continued. It took about thirty seconds for the congregation to realise that the sound would not abate and that they heard the sound of the mine whistle.

The most dreaded noise that summoned every available man back to the colliery, it was a sound that guaranteed tragedy.

The organ stopped abruptly. The eerie silence in the church was palpable as everybody held their breath to listen.

There was not a sound except for the sharp note from the shrill whistle. Even the gale had stopped to pay attention.

To the congregation, the significance of the sound was profound. The church erupted into chaos. The men ran back down the aisle and poured out through the great chapel doors. In their haste, male members of the choir had discarded their robes and left them on the floor tiles to gather grubby footprints and trip the unwary.

The men ran down the hill toward the mine, ungainly arms flailing, heels of their hobnailed boots skidding down the sloping, rain-soaked terrain. The pit was made of dark shadows in the gloom.

Behind them followed the women, gathering up their skirts, lungs burning with the uncustomary effort. Behind them were the children tumbling and bouncing unaware of the crushing truth, under the watchful gaze of the portly minister -- who had suddenly found himself without a congregation.

"Derryn," cried Bronwyn "my William is down there. He's only fifteen."

"Tiny will have kept an eye on him. I am sure," yelled Derryn over the din.

"Can you remember which level he was working on?" Bronwyn shrieked back.

"Two," replied Derryn.

"Yes, Willy as well."

"Oh, dear, God, where is Rebecca?" shouted Derryn.

"She'll follow, Derryn. Keep going, I am sure that Reverend Hughes will bring her down."

"You think?"

"Yes. Of course."

They looked behind and saw a red-faced reverend bringing up the rear.

As the two women fled towards the opening to the shaft, they were both filled with dread at the possibility it could be one of their own.

2

THE RESCUE

The first thing the men noted was that the sheave wheel had stopped turning, which meant they were no longer winching people to the surface. The shrill whistle continued to scream and grate on everyone's raw nerves, adding to their anxiety levels and exacerbating the confusion.

George Watkins could only imagine the chaos down below whether fire, water, or collapse, the chances were high that there was certain death. George was a head taller than the crowd and could see a well-dressed man climb onto a platform near the entrance to the mine. He recognised him as Graham Griffiths, the mine manager. Mr Griffiths was no miner, of that George was sure. Mr Griffiths sat in his office all day, his desk was piled with books, and he was notorious for handing out unreasonable tasks and targets as he sat like a lord, but this was how it worked. The manager, regardless of the lack of practical experience, would stand on the podium announce the emergency and then he would return at whatever hour it was that the men were hauled to the service and he would report the deaths.

"Ladies and gentleman, there is no need to panic," said Mr Griffiths. He was a hazy figure in the depressing mid-morning twilight. He picked up his bullhorn and addressed the crowd, his speech short.

 "There has been a collapse on the level-" He stopped to try and tame the piece of paper flapping in his hand. Finally, regaining control, he continued.

"Level two. The seam where the collapse occurred had four people working in it. A search has commenced. We hope to have more information for you as soon as possible. There is no need to panic."

The words were always the same, business-like and efficient. He spoke as though he was reading from a newspaper, not addressing a crowd of walking, talking, feeling humans; it reminded George that he was a mere employee, a servant to the master. If he were honest with himself, he was more of a slave. His weekly wage was just enough to trap him. It barely put food on the family table, so without his son's weekly wages, the family would starve. He couldn't demand better wage, lodgings or better working hours, because there were many men desperate for work and ready to take his job, however terrible the working conditions.

Filled with fury, George wondered how many more times would men die because it cost too much to implement basic safety practices. Mr Griffiths was happy to do the bare minimum.

Death by suffocation was almost inevitable in an underground accident, whatever the root cause. How many times would he have to hear the same cold, routine speech over and over? It was so ingrained in his memory that Mr Griffiths dramatic announcement was unnecessary-he could match his delivery word for word.

George knew that now it was just a matter of waiting. The miners in the pit would not leave until they had recovered the bodies of their friends. They would work as a team to physically dig out their colleagues or even their children.

He had seen grown men on their hands and knees weeping, while they dug out the dead with their bare hands. Occasionally, there was a miracle, and somebody survived, but George would never wager a bet on it.

Women with no family members underground shuffled back to their cottages to take care of their families and the children who had mothers or fathers standing at the pit mouth, desperate for news. Alice had tried to escort Becca from the scene, but she was adamant she wanted to stay with her mother. The rest of the miners' families set up a vigil at the shaft waiting for news and praying that their child, husband or father was not a victim of injury or death. Becca clung tightly to her mother's coat-clad leg.

It was during the early hours of the following morning that the anxious crowd finally got the update they craved and dreaded.

The colliers that braved the danger of the rescue had been underground for almost eighteen hours, by now they would be shocked, exhausted and no doubt grieving for the loss of their brethren.

Events like this galvanised the men creating explicit factions between the workers and the owners. At the same time, the Union leaders took advantage of the opportunity to further their political agenda.

George Watkins could see activity at the shaft, and the big iron wheel began to turn. The cage was lifting men—live or dead—from the blackness.

The elusive Mr Griffiths stepped out of the main building, walked across the yard. With some difficulty, he climbed up onto the back of a cart which now served as a makeshift podium. The murmuring crowd hushed as he raised the bullhorn to his mouth.

"Unfortunately," he began, giving the miners a foretaste of what was to come, "a collapse underground has resulted in one death, but we have saved two lives." The crowd clapped softly, for the rescuers, not the cowardly Griffiths. "We share our commiserations with the family of the deceased," Griffiths consoled, trying to sound vaguely compassionate. "In light of the tragedy, we have lost many hours of production. As you know, we have had to offer overtime to keep up with demand. Please report to your charter master, we will be working a double shift for the rest of the week."

Mr Griffiths couldn't get his rotund body off the wagon. He had to be assisted by the men he exploited. George and many other lads had the desire to go up to the front and wallop the insensitive fellow in his fat face. George had seen many riots erupt when callous managers made insensitive remarks. Mr Griffiths was lucky that the crowd was not in that mood today.

Derryn seemed to have developed a sixth sense. Her skin began to tingle. The hair on her neck stood up, and she felt a wave of nausea rise up from her clenched belly. Somehow, she knew in her bones that Tiny was dead.

She ran to the front of the crowd and George watched the crowd part like the Red Sea as she moved through it, Becca tottering a few paces behind.

"Oh, dear God," he thought, "please don't let it be Tiny. They are such good, honest people."

"My Tiny was on level two, George! Please tell me he's safe."

George knew the young man well, and his small daughter whom he often saw out and about the village with her mother doing errands. He often smiled as he saw them sat talking, taking in the views from the hillside on warm Saturday evenings. He didn't know how Tiny's wife would take the news, but he felt desperately sorry for them both.

The cage surfaced, and the two survivors were the first to be delivered to safety - Sean Carlisle, a fifteen-year-old lad, who came from an old mining family, followed by Willy Brown, Bronwyn and Edwyn's boy.

Bronwyn's face lit up with relief when she saw her son escorted out of the mine by his father. She ran toward them and broke into tears, the three of them huddled in an embrace. Bronwyn gently punched Willy on his arm.

"What are you doing terrifying your poor mother like that?"

She hugged him tightly and wouldn't release him for a long time.

As she passed them, Derryn heard the words "Tiny saved us, Ma, he saved our lives."

The last victim was carried out, his face was covered by a dirty brown jacket, but Derryn recognized the lunch box that lay on the stretcher next to him. It was a reminder of the last good meal that she would ever provide for her husband.

A tired and hungry Becca followed her mother through the murmuring crowd, baffled, not understanding the significance of the moment they were about to face.

The oil lights shone dully about them. Becca glanced down, saw with horror that there was black mud at the bottom of her mum's church dress which lodged in her little mind as more of a tragedy than the death of her father.

Derryn reached the stretcher and slowly lifted up the coat not sure what state he would be in. *If he is too gruesome, some kind soul will stop me, surely.* Underneath the fabric emerged the peaceful face of her husband. Someone had wiped the coal dust from it to make an accurate identification at the scene. There was no mistaking her husband for anyone else - or that the Lord had chosen to cut short his life that day.

She saw her daughter's head peer around the jacket, then turn up to face her.

"Is he dead, Ma?" asked Becca, with the frankness that only a child could get away with.

"Yes," answered Derryn, in barely a whisper, before turning to the men with the stretcher.

"Will you please take him home for me?"

"Course we will, Miss," answered one of the bearers.

Derryn looked across at Bronwyn, still clutching her husband and son, and temporarily, she was filled with bitterness. Fuelled by resentment, in her grief, her mind began to fill with questions and accusations. *How dare Willy to be saved. Did he cause the Tiny's death playing the fool? He was fond of larking about. Why has God punished me?* Ultimately, her feelings pivoted on one question. *Why did your child live and my husband die?*

3

FOLLOWING THE STRETCHER

Derryn escorted the stretcher up the hill to her cottage. She held Becca's hand on one side, and the other held the cold, dead, stiffening hand of Tiny. They lifted her husband's body onto the table with as much dignity as they could muster and lay him down gently while Derryn and Becca looked on.

"Why won't me Da' wake up?" asked Becca, but Derryn didn't have an answer for her, and the small child sat in bewilderment watching the activity taking place around her.

She was filled with confusion and insecurity because nothing seemed reasonable. Why were all these people in her house, why was her mother crying, her mother never cried,

why were they up in the middle of the night,
why were they all dressed in day clothes?

Sadly, she had heard others talk about death, but the cruel definition behind it was something she was yet to learn first-hand.

Derryn looked at Tiny, her mind flitted between acceptance that he was dead, and hope that he may wake up, then back to acceptance and then disbelief that he was dead, stone dead without any possibility of being his warm, living self again.

In the pandemonium, three old women of the village arrived, they were all dressed in black and descended upon the small cottage like crows.

"Derryn, we are here to help you," said Efa
Brown.

She was known to be the oldest woman in the village, nobody knew exactly how many years she was, but her face befitted the legend. She had two old women with her, but Derryn didn't have the energy to remember their names or speak to them.

Efa Brown told her that it was vital for the sake of Tiny's soul that they guide her through the rituals of preparing the dead for burial. Derryn had never had to bury anybody before and was relieved that somebody was on hand to assist. The unannounced visit was welcome.

Efa Brown looked at the sight around her. The cottage was neat as a pin but cold.

"Get a fire going," she ordered.

Tiny's body still lay on the table under the dirty coat, now some hours after his death. They would have to work quickly.

Becca sat on Derryn's lap on the rocking chair, soaking in the warmth from the neighbouring stove. Becca took in everything that was happening around her with great interest. Nobody was particularly worried about the child being there or what she saw, mining was an occupation peppered by work and death, and the two couldn't be separated. Mining was generational, and the chances that Becca would be a miner's wife was high. Inevitably, this was just the first of many repeat experiences she would suffer.

Efa Brown called for clean cloths and carbolic soap. One woman worked with Efa washing the body and the third boiled and filled basins with water. Derryn couldn't stop looking at Tiny. He lay peacefully and was probably laughing at the scene below. Derryn could imagine him saying—*if I had known I would have so many women fiddling with me, I would've died sooner.*

She watched them remove his clothes. They unbuttoned his shirt revealing the chest she had laid her head against every night, listening to his steady heartbeat, with his miner's strong, muscular arms surrounding her—comforting her. His gnarled hands would touch her like she was a delicate flower. She had fallen in love with his good looks and roguish, flirtatious smile the moment she saw him merrymaking with his chums at the local eisteddfod. She found it amusing they called him Tiny, despite his tall stature and athletic build.

Eventually, her husband's lifeless body was naked. Oil of camphor was added into some water to keep his skin soft and repel the insects, then they washed his stiff body from top to bottom. After his front was finished, they rolled him onto his stomach and did the back of him. The final stage was done on his side. Efa began washing his hair. Derryn set down her daughter gently, got up and walked to the table. The young widow touched his hand, then stared at his face. Alas, try as she may, she couldn't will him back to life.

Becca dragged a chair next to her mother and climbed onto the hard-wooden seat. She looked at her father with some curiosity.

"He smells very clean, Ma." said the ever-practical little voice.

Efa Brown and her friends began to wrap Tiny in a white sheet. They started at his feet and twisted crisp cotton cloth around him until his face was covered.

Derryn moved closer to Becca and put her arm around the child.

"He's not going to wake up, is he, Ma?"

Derryn bit hard into her stiffening lower lip so hard it tingled, then shook her head.

"Will he go to heaven, Ma?"

"Of course," replied Derryn.

"You don't have to worry about that dwti, he will be in heaven," reassured Efa Brown. "We will send for Ludnow Gravis to make sure of it."

Derryn spun around and looked at the old woman.

"Are you sure?" She asked in a low voice. "I don't believe in it."

"Of course, I am sure, are you prepared to take the risk? You are not from these hills, are you?" asked Efa forcefully.

"No," answered Derryn.

Derryn looked at the floor, she couldn't meet the woman's eyes, she was torn between fear and faith. If she agreed to the suggestion, she was bound to face criticism from the villagers and if she declined, Tiny might be damned to eternal hell. Efa Brown was a commanding personality, and Derryn, intimidated by the woman, didn't dare to face up to her. Young, vulnerable and afraid of the assertive older woman, eventually, Derryn nodded her head in surrender.

"Tidy then, Derryn," said Efa. "At least you'll have peace, everybody who has called on the man's service says they havc pcace."

"Ma! Ma!" nagged Becca, "who is —L—?"

This time, Derryn didn't finish the sentence.

"Ludnow Gravis?" volunteered Efa Brown.

"Enough, Becca," growled Derryn. "Go to the bedroom."

"But who is he?"

Before Derryn could shoo her away to the room, Efa Brown took over yet again.

"He's the sin-eater, child."

4

THE MEDDLESOME
EFA BROWN

Efa Brown could find nobody willing to take a message to Ludnow Gravis at his farm and early on the Monday morning eventually she had to pay the local postmaster to deliver him a note.

"Efa Brown, no!" warned Edward Purvis, the postmaster. "Those times are behind us, Efa. I haven't seen Ludnow up here doing that for about a year now. It is the old ways. This is a bad thing that you are doing. Leave the man in peace won't you?"

"And do you want the poor man's soul resting on your conscience for all eternity Edward?" rasped Efa. "Tiny could have done no repenting, not in that circus that was happening around him underground. No, he likely didna even think of offering a prayer for his soul like. And he wasn't a staunch churchman. I know that. Never saw him in the church, I didn't."

"What did young Derryn say about all this?"

"Of course, she agreed like, I had no problem, in fact, it was her idea."

"I'm sure you don't need reminding Efa, nobody is going to like this. It's going to bring up a lot of anger now after all the time. The young generation don't do this anymore, and I am surprised Derryn agreed, she being so young an' all."

"Stop chopsing, Edward. Just send the lad down there. My money is good, and I'm paying ye. Don't you argue now?"

A further burden landed in Edward's lap. Efa's illiteracy meant he had to write the note to Ludnow Gravis himself. He folded up her request he gave it to the young post boy, Harry, who pulled a face when he saw the name and address.

"Now wait a minute, Sir," grumbled Harry. "I don't like going down that way, and you know why!"

"Just deliver the damn thing and be done with it. Do you think I like the bloody idea meself?" Edward complained.

The post lad noticed that Edward had cursed twice in one sentence. *Efa Brown has him tamping.*

"The man is strange, yes, Harry. But he has lived on that farm for many years, and he is harmless. Do you hear me? Harmless."

"I don't want to say this, Sir, but he is not friendly when I drop the post. Nigh on ignores me," grizzled the irate assistant.

"Yes, Ludnow has his demons. I don't know what they are, but they are there. He started off alright, mind." explained Edward. "Went to school here. Very clever fellow, so they say. Brilliant, in fact. Won a scholarship, he did, then went to university in England an all. Became an engineer, if I recall right."

Edward gazed into the distance remembering the past.

"The villagers were so proud of him, but he returned, and he was different." sighed Edward.

Nothing that Edward said made young Harry feel better about making the delivery.

"He behaves older, but he is only about thirty-five. When he came back here about ten years ago, that is when he started this strange business that he does. Could have a

high paying position on the mine, he could.
But he stays out on that farm bordering the
woods. Just him all by himself. Nobody has
ever been in the house."

Edward was talking to himself now. Harry was too
fed up to listen.

"It's a mystery why he does what he does.
When he comes in here, he is decent. He has
a good livestock business over there, I
think—but he doesn't talk. Keeps himself to
himself."

"Strange, if ya ask me," muttered Harry.

"And who asked you, boy? Just take the note
and stop ya back chat, hear? He has to be up
by Derryn today, so hurry up," thundered
Edward.

"Yes, Sir, Yes, Sir. Three bags full, Sir!" said
Harry under his breath.

The boy got on his boneshaker of a bicycle and rode
away like the devil was behind him. Instead of taking
his usual route towards the mine, Harry veered off in
another direction. He followed a winding road
through the trees to the far edge of the nearby
woodland. On a typical day, it would have been a
beautiful ride through the countryside, but as he
approached the desolate dwelling, he shuddered. It
was as if someone was walking over his grave.

The stable-style door to Derryn's cottage was open, and Efa Brown was leaning on the bottom half waiting for the hotly anticipated arrival of Ludnow Gravis. He would know the urgency. It was Monday afternoon, and Tiny's body had to be in the grave by Tuesday afternoon. The undertaker would bring down the coffin in the morning because it would be a struggle to get through the cottage door and into the tiny kitchen. The coroner would lift Tiny off the table and place him into the coffin. Efa knew what she was doing. She would insist that they carry him feet first, so there was no way he could look back, and then she would instruct them to walk the long route to the church so that his ghost couldn't find his way home again.

The day had gone by with a constant stream of visitors.

Bronwyn arrived to see Efa Brown leaning out the door.

"Afternoon, Efa. Is Derryn in?" enquired a softly spoken Bronwyn.

"In the bed with the lil' one," snapped Efa. She wasn't particularly fond of Bronwyn, a woman she felt was overly bold and couldn't be intimidated easily.

Bronwyn sidled past the old crone and walked into the tiny room that served as a bedroom. An iron bed dominated the cramped space, the walls were uneven but clean, and the bedclothes were spotless. Becca lay next to her mother, fast asleep.

"Right, Derryn, how are you fettling?" asked her friend.

"Tired. Numb." answered Derryn, "I wish all these people would just get out of my house now."

"I see Efa has done Tiny," said Bronwyn quietly.

"Yes, yes, I was in there when they were busy."

Bronwyn nodded, "what time is the service?"

"The minister was here just after we brought Tiny home, we've settled on two o'clock tomorrow afternoon."

"The girls down the row are putting some food together for afterwards," said Bronwyn.

Derryn nodded her thanks. Bronwyn sat on the bed and held her friend's hand.

"Derryn, if it could have been another way, I mean, my Willy is alright like, but I cannot help but feel guilty cos Tiny died down there helping my boy, oh Derryn, I am so sorry." Bronwyn burst into tears.

Derryn clamped her hand over Bronwyn's.

"It's alright Bronwyn, it's alright it is. It was the way Tiny was. It was his choice to help them. It's been a terrible blow, but I know in your heart Bronwyn—" she couldn't finish the sentence.

"Is anybody staying here tonight?" asked Bronwyn. "You can't be alone."

"Nah, Nah, I'll be fine on my own like. I want to be alone. Efa has got Ludnow Gravis coming sometime today. I do hope it will not be too late." sighed Derryn.

"Derryn!" Bronwyn exclaimed, "why do you want somebody like that up here in yer house? Those days are over Derryn, we don't do that anymore, it's a dark practice. Derryn, you can't be having that man in your house near yer child. I'm going to Efa now to put a stop to all this nonsense right now."

"I am too tired to fight," sighed Derryn. "I just didn't have the strength to argue."

"You know the villagers are going to be hopping mad, now, don't you? Does Reverend Hughes know about this? He'll be livid."

Derryn shook her head and looked at the entwined hands.

"Just let it be Bronwyn, please just let it be. But will yer stay, please?"

"There is going to be quite a crowd gathering out there when they see him. You know nothing of these old Welsh ways, you coming from the city and all," Bronwyn said, shaking her head.

Both women were quiet for a while, in their own worlds. Then, Bronwyn suddenly snapped out of her reverie and nodded.

"Yes, I'll stay, of course, I'll stay."

"Bronwyn, who is this man, Ludnow Gravis?"

"He's somebody that lived here in the village a long time ago. I remember him from when he was wee lad," replied Bronwyn.

"No, Bronwyn. I mean this job of his? What does he do?"

"He is called a Sin-Eater, Derryn. He takes upon himself the sins of the man who has died. It's an old ritual, not popular with young people, but the old crones like Efa Brown still keep it going."

"And this Gravis man, how did—" she tried to find the right words. "how did he become this 'sin thing', Bronwyn?"

"I don't know his story Derryn. Most villagers just stay away. They are suspicious. Loathe him, they do. You will see."

5

THE SUMMONING OF LUDNOW GRAVIS

Ludnow Gravis arrived on foot, and by the time he reached the colliery, he already had a few people following him. He was hunched over from the cold and had put his hands into his coat pockets to keep himself warm. He wore a long brown coat which reached mid-thigh and a pair of well-worn boots that stretched to above his knees. He wore a black trilby that hid his face, and his hunched shadowy figure could be seen coming up the hill in the gloom. Ludnow was a tall man, probably six foot and three inches. His shoulders were broad as a man who toiled at the coalface every day. His brown hair was long, almost to his shoulders. His face was hidden by a neat short beard. His piercing blue eyes saw everything around him, yet gave away nothing. Nobody got the privilege of seeing the soul dwelling inside the body.

Derryn looked on down the road toward him, there were about twenty people about him now, shouting insults.

"Get away from our village Gravis," yelled a collier.

"You are bringing the devil with you, Gravis! Go home."

"Go do yer evil in another place, we don't want you about our women and children."

"Let the dead be, get away from here, go."

The abuse was not part of the ritual, but it was part of the process.

Although Bronwyn had warned Derryn, she hadn't imagined that there would be such a confrontation between Ludnow and the villagers.

George Watkins watched the figure turn up the lane into the Collier's Row, then he noticed Efa Brown open the door and stand in front of it like an evil beacon. In his opinion, Efa was much more sinister than Ludnow could ever be. *So, this is all old Efa Brown's doing*? He had lived in these rows all his life, and he had witnessed her malevolence over the years. He knew without a doubt that today was no different. He put on his hat and began to walk toward Ludnow Gravis. When George reached the man,

Gravis doffed his hat in acknowledgement. George greeted the man with kindness.

"Hello, Son. Here, I'll accompany you up the lane if you'll allow me?"

Gravis nodded.

"Are you well?"

"Yes, Mr Watkins, thank you."

"You don't have to do this Ludnow, this here thing, it's old ways Son, you don't have to do this for no one."

He nodded.

There was a braying mob of people hurling abuse at Gravis, but nobody was brave enough to get too close to him.

George walked as far as Efa Brown at the cottage door, and he stopped before her "This is the last time you do this Efa Brown, do you hear me, this is the last time that you torment this man, the last time."

Efa Brown swore under her breath just loud enough for George to hear, but he stood his ground, not leaving Ludnow's side.

"Bronwyn, what are the troubles out there?" asked Derryn.

"Yes, George knew the family for a long time. I am glad George is taking on old Efa. Like a witch she is. She has evil in her, Derryn. More devilish than Gravis. Three hundred years ago Efa would have been burnt as a witch."

"Oh, Bronwyn, I didn't know this would cause so much trouble. I only vaguely knew what it was. What have I done?"

Ludnow nodded at Efa Brown, who opened the door wider to allow him through it into the house. He took off his hat and stepped inside. There was a lamp burning in the room which cast long shadows against the walls. A woman was standing with a small girl in the far corner, at first, he thought it was the widow. Still, when he became accustomed to the light he recognised Bronwyn, his gaze continued to travel around the room, there was a table with the body on it and next to the table stood a young woman of about twenty-five. He caught himself staring at her for longer than he needed to, she was stunning, and her blonde hair caught the light of the lamp, and it shone gold like a halo around her head. She was of average height, and even standing at the far end of the table, her posture defeated, slumped, he saw that she had all the curves that men dream about.

She greeted him by looking straight into his eyes, fearlessly and nodded. The eyes held no judgement or condemnation, in fact, there was a kindness in them that surprised him, he became embarrassed.

He dropped his eyes to the ground as he moved toward the table for his beggar's feast.

He looked at the body on the table. *So, this was the man privileged to have such a beautiful wife.*

The body was washed and wrapped in a clean white sheet, yet still, he could smell the camphor that it had been rinsed with. On the corpse's chest was a bowl filled with salt. On top of that, rested a chunk of bread. Ludnow took a chair and turned it toward the door and sat down. Without a single word, Efa Brown knew it was time to put money into his palm, and the ceremony began. He slowly stood up and lifted the dish off the cadaver, then sat down again and slowly started eating the bread.

Derryn watched him closely as he broke off one piece of bread at a time. He could have swallowed it in a moment, but he took his time. There was a humility about the sacrament, and being so close, she could see his eyes well up with tears. Derryn forgot her own sorrow for a moment and was filled with the most overwhelming pity for the man, she also wanted to cry, but not for her husband, for the tortured man that was Ludnow. He finished the bread and Efa handed him a glass of beer that he drank quickly as if to say 'it is over.' He stood up, moved to the table and hovered over the corpse. Derryn had the perception that the handful of onlookers were disappearing into the dark shadows of the small room. Some people covered their faces.

Others turned to face the wall, the reluctance to observe the ritual too distressing to bear.

Ludnow began to talk over the dead man, his hands hovering above the sheet.

"I give you peace and rest."

He paused and took a deep breath,

"Do not come back to this village, or its lanes or its fields. For your peace, I take upon me your sins and trade my soul."

"No!" Derryn protested.

Ludnow turned around. Derryn knew if the sin-eater could really absolve her husband of any wrong-doings, there would be many to atone for. Tiny was never a regular churchgoer, preferring rest on a Sunday rather than repentance with Reverend Hughes.

"The ceremony is complete. Tiny has gone to a better place, my dear. It is over," whispered Efa Brown.

Derryn was crying, heartbroken on his behalf. She stared straight at him as she reprimanded the superstitious old woman:

"Efa! How could you make him do this terrible thing to himself?"

"Be still, Derryn. Calm yourself. Think of the girl."

Ludnow looked at Derryn and their eyes connected. This time he didn't turn away and held her gaze for what seemed like minutes. He noticed her eyes were filled with deep compassion and humiliation. She could hardly speak. The guilt and need to atone burned her throat so much clamped her silent voice box.

"I am so sorry," she mouthed.

"I know," he replied softly. "I know."

6

THE CHURCH ON THE HILL

Tiny was buried up on the hill by the church. The body was carried feet first from the house, and the long trail of mourners followed behind it, led by Derryn and Becca. The choir sang so powerfully, it was as though the voices alone could lift the spirit of the dead man to the doors of heaven. Flowers covered the coffin with the mining company providing the biggest wreath with the most ribbons. Derryn thought it was ironic that the flowers were probably worth a month's wage. *It was money they should have given to the living to improve the safety, instead of lamenting the dead.*

Becca stood next to Derryn, and she held the child's hand tightly as if terrified that physically letting go in that moment meant losing her too. Becca made her own observations. She could sense her mother was not fully present. The hand squeeze was affectionate, but she seemed distant, detached from the rest of the world. Becca sensed the detachment, and she felt alone amongst the huddle of strangers. The five-year-old girl began to holler at the top of her voice. It was not the loss of her father that incited it, but the perception that now, she was losing her mother too.

The mourners lined up to offer their condolences to Derryn and Becca. First came Mr Griffiths who promised to look after her and insisted she should not worry about anything. He advised her that on Friday she was to go to his office and they would discuss the future. Tiny's colleagues followed, a long stream of men that she had never met before, and probably would never meet again, offered their condolences in the kindest possible way. Lastly, their friends and neighbours engulfed her with kind words and offers of assistance if she needed any. Derryn nodded her head in thanks, feeling in a daze. Everything around her was a blur of people and voices. Nothing was tangible. Later that afternoon, she couldn't tell you who she had spoken to. She was neither happy nor sad. She functioned more as an observer than a participant. A numbness had settled over her emotions, and she felt no ache of loss. She couldn't evoke the emotional display necessary to qualify as a grieving widow.

The coffin was lowered into the ground in the dark gloom of the afternoon. Lamps had been lit in the cemetery to mark the path of the coffin and their dull glow ineffective. Light would never claim victory over the darkness of this day.

The mourners walked by the grave, and each threw in a woody sprig of rosemary. A handful of wet soil followed. Bronwyn watched as Mr Griffiths put a silver coin on the shovel of a gravedigger. At least this time, his generosity would benefit the living.

Bronwyn took Becca's arm as they left the graveyard, and the people followed them. There would be food and drink at the cottage, and later most of the people would move the party to the pub.

Derryn wished they would all go away, she wanted to be alone. She desperately wanted to scrub the cottage and remove the smell of the camphor that would always remind her of death from that day forward. Then she tried to wash, and after that, she wanted to sit next to the warm fire, drink tea and just be.

Lost in her thoughts, she stared into the distance. Still, her imagination was disturbed by a moving shadow, a figure, at the edge of the woodland. There was a flash, and then it was gone. She could have sworn that it was Ludnow Gravis.

The next day, Derryn had resumed cleaning her bedroom when there was a knock at the door.

"I'll open, I'll open," shouted Becca, eager to have a visitor.

"Yes, that is a tidy area. Can you open the door, my little flower?"

Becca stood on her tiptoes and pulled the handle down. She gave it a pull and almost lost her balance as the door swung open on its creaky hinges.

"Hello, Becca!" said Reverend Hughes, followed by a big smile. "Where is your Ma, little one?"

"She is in the bedroom," answered the child, wanting to look organised and grown-up. "I will call her here if you like."

"Ma," she yelled at the top of her voice, "the churchman has paid us a visit."

Reverend Hughes looked around the room as he waited. The cottage was small, humble, and immaculate. There were a few cheery pictures hung against the wall and a colourful knotted-rag rug on the rough stone floor to provide a little comfort to bare feet. Pretty crockery was stacked on a polished wooden dresser. The room had a welcoming atmosphere.

Derryn walked into the small kitchen, and despite feeling annoyed at the interruption, greeted the minister with a faint smile.

"Hello, Reverend. And how are you today?" she asked dutifully.

"Very well thank you," said Reverend Hughes, his accent confirming his educated and privileged background. "It's a lovely little place you have here. It is very homely compared to some of the other cottages."

It was meant as a compliment, but it irritated her.

"I was expecting you to have a house full of mourners," it was a statement, not a rhetorical question.

"I asked them to leave, Reverend. The house was full of people. I know they meant well, but I couldn't find my peace."

"Mmm, I think the service went very well yesterday Derryn, Tiny was a popular man around here."

"Would you like some tea, Reverend?" she asked, not wanting to discuss Tiny with him. She wasn't ready to expose that raw wound to anybody else.

"Thank you. You're too kind, Mrs Evans," he replied.

"So, how long have you known Efa Brown, Derryn?" inquired the clergyman.

Derryn knew that there had to be an ulterior motive for the visit from the moment she had seen him at her front door.

"I have seen her in the village. I only met her properly in the early hours of the morning on the day when Tiny—" she swallowed to try and loosen the words in her throat, "—when Tiny passed. She came to help me prepare him for the funeral. Clean him up."

The reverend sat on the chair with one leg crossed over the other in a feminine manner and nodded, taking in all the details to make a judgement. He took a sip of his tea then peered at her over the rim of the cup.

"Do you happen to know a fellow called Ludnow Gravis?"

She knew the point he was driving towards and cut to the chase hoping it would curtail the unannounced and unwanted visit.

"No, t'was the first time I met him," she said flatly.

He nodded again, and they sat in an uncomfortable silence for a while.

"What did you think of him? You know that he is a pariah in this village?"

Derryn could do nothing but be honest.

"In truth, Reverend, I felt very sorry for him," she explained.

The minister's eyes widened, and his voice rose.

"How could you feel sorry for that monster? You saw what that heretic did with your own eyes - and you still managed to feel sorry for him?"

The widow's annoyance bled into her choice of words.

"Yes, I felt huge compassion for him. He was so tortured as if his tragedy was greater than mine."

"Have you lost your mind? The devil clearly lives within him. He is straight from the bowels of hell," snarled the reverend, his voice filled with anger, judgement, fire and brimstone.

"He is filled with the evil of all the men whom he has exorcised. You should never have allowed him over the threshold. We must sprinkle this house with holy water and incense after his satanic practices."

Derryn was losing her temper. Who was this stranger to come into her home and question her actions and impregnate her with fear? *I did my best to care for Tiny, in life as I did in death.*

"I don't think that needs to happen, Reverend. Ludnow Gravis didn't seem like a monster to me."

"How dare you decide the likes of good and evil? You have never studied scripture. How can he have consumed your husband's sins? The corrupt days of paying for religious indulgences to guarantee salvation ended with the dissolution of the monasteries."

"You can believe what you like, judge me as harshly as you wish. I did my duty and cared for my husband on his final journey underground."

The minister was aghast, it was not often that he suffered rebuke, most people allowed him into their home, welcomed being patronised. This woman, clearly a non-conformist in the reverend's mind, had caught him off guard.

His preferred manipulation strategy was not going to work with her, so he decided to soften his approach.

"I know, I know, but the—let's call it gentleness—of the man, has obviously closed your spiritual eyes to the terrible threat he represents to our community. Please be careful and diligently repent in your daily

prayers--for allowing the devil's advocate
into your once happy home."

She looked at him with sickening disgust. Ludnow
had provided a degree of solace more than both the
mine owner and orthodox church combined.

"I will not repent. All he wanted to do was to
ease my suffering!" she countered.

For Derryn, that was not enough, though. Incensed,
she had one last question aimed squarely at the
clergyman's theological jugular vein:

"What kind of church is it that cannot love
thy neighbour? What kind of holy man are
you, Reverend?"

The minister had no answer to that. The widow was
strong and self-assured, and she was right. He could
find no logical or spiritual answer to justify
ostracising the man. He should be viewed as a lost
sheep in need of salvation, not a demon. Hughes felt
some sympathy with her position, even if he had no
stomach to support it.

"Thank you for the tea, Derryn," he said with an
overly polite smile. "Will I see you in church on
Sunday? The choir is all the better with your vocal
accompaniment."

She didn't reply but opened the door for him. The
minister left with his cassock between his legs.

7

THE MEETING WITH MR GRIFFITHS

Derryn and Becca made their way to the colliery for a meeting with Mr Griffiths, the mine manager. George Watkins had quietly advised her to be firm with him and not to be intimidated.

> "Derryn," he said kindly, "We have unions that protect workers. If Griffiths tries any funny business, you have recourse to the law. He is a forceful young man in his early thirties. Do not be afraid of him. Stand up for your rights. Don't accept the offer if the figures don't add up."

Derryn took a deep breath, and as her lungs expanded, she felt her stiff corset, like life itself, try to constrain her—keep her in her place. Becca fidgeted. Being dragged along on errands always brought out her impatience.

Stood by the frosted glass door, Derryn peered through the transparent portions which made up the word 'OFFICE'.

She could make out a lone man in a dark suit sat at a desk lit from the side by a big window. Her firm knock was not graced with a reply. After a few nervous moments, she took the door handle and gave it a determined twist. She walked into the room and was relieved to see that the fire was glowing. *At least some physical warmth to this place.*

Derryn introduced herself to the clerk. When he stood in surprise to greet her, she noted he was an unusually tall man, perhaps even taller than Ludnow. When he sat behind the wooden desk Becca wondered how his long legs managed to fit underneath it. Behind him, there were matching wooden shelves, burgeoning with box files. He looked ancient. His silvery grey hair was combed straight back, and a thick coating of shiny cream kept it so flat it hugged his scalp. He had a hooked nose and mischievous eyes. Becca liked his curious countenance immediately.

"Mrs Evans!" he said with a huge smile. "I am Mr Crowsen. I've been expecting you. And you have brought young Miss Evans with you, I see."

"Yes," answered Derryn with a cheeriness that surprised her.

The man's happiness was infectious. She had no choice but to smile in return, despite the maudlin circumstances underpinning her visit. His warm and polite attitude was a welcome relief to Reverend Hughes's dressing down attempt the day before.

Becca's impatience had turned into tardiness yet again. Derryn had to take the girl's weight by pulling her arm up above her waist. The child had no choice but to tiptoe along beside.

"I must apologise. Mr Griffiths is going to be a short while yet. Would you like some tea?" He volunteered.

"Oh, yes, please!" replied Becca.

Derryn could have died with embarrassment and wanted to give her a clip round the ear.

"Don't be forward," she chastised the child.

"Of course. I will make you some tea," the assistant obliged, smiling at Becca. "And, can I give you a biscuit as well, Miss? Would you like that?"

"Yes please, Sir," answered Becca, remembering her manners. She was delighted with the man who was rapidly becoming her new best friend.

Derryn had just finished her tea when Mr Crowsen announced that Mr Griffiths would see her.

"Now young Miss Evans, would you like to draw me a picture of your mother while she talks to the manager?"

He gestured to a fresh piece of paper, and a sharpened pencil and invited the girl to sit down.

"It's ok, Ma, you can go," said Becca, her desire for independence stinging her mother's heart once more.

Tentatively, her sense of isolation growing, Derryn made her way towards the closed door to the right, with 'General Manager' etched into the glass. Another deep breath later, and she found herself in front of Griffiths.

"Good morning, Mrs Evans," greeted the manager.

"Mr Griffiths."

He shook her hand and gave it an unwelcome and inappropriate stroke with his fat forefinger. He had taken a good look at her. She didn't qualify as the average miners' wife. There was an unusual air of style and class about her, alluded to by her well-spoken tone. His eyes lingered over her, and as his gaze broke, she could sense he was carefully undressing her, his lustful imagination enjoying every moment. Derryn felt sick that her fate was under this odious man's control.

Although young, Mr Griffiths was already balding. His gingery hair was desperately old fashioned, trimmed into the same style as a medieval monk. His pink, hairless face had been rounded over the years by over-indulgence. Two yellowing buck teeth just managed to protrude from his small slit of a mouth. His worst feature by far, for Derryn, was his hands. His fingers were as fat as pork sausages, and his nails were bitten to the quick. Finally, he relinquished his insidious stroking grasp.

"Now my dear," he began, "the owner and I are devastated by the loss of your beloved husband, Tony—" he said with mock humility.

"—Tiny," corrected Derryn. "But thank you."

"Of course, you must know your husband had an insurance fund which was administrated by the Sibb's Mining Company."

Derryn nodded.

"Based on the contributions, there is a payment due to you of, let me see—"

He traced his finger down one of the two sheets of paper on his desk.

"—twenty-four shillings—"

Derryn look horrified, feeling utterly cheated at the pitifully small level of remuneration compared to the hefty dues the family had regularly paid in for several years.

"I do beg your pardon, Mrs Evans, that should be twenty-four pounds, ten shillings and thruppence. It is deemed this amount will be enough to sustain you for a minimum of six months."

"Thank you very much," she said with relief.

"Now, there is just a little matter of signing the paperwork. Can you write?"

Derryn felt insulted by the question. She nodded, giving him a furious stare at the same time.

"Please do take a seat."

Griffiths gave her an odd frown and walked behind the wide desk then pushed the two documents in front of her. As he returned to her side of the table, he began to elaborate, in an irritating, patronising tone.

"Let me explain them to you, my dear."

Derryn flinched when he tried to brush his right hand across her bosom as he bent over to reach the left-most piece of paperwork. With her eyes almost in line with his waistband, she noticed that for him, this secret thrill had manifested itself as a sickening bulge underneath his buttoned fly. Disgusted, she dragged her heavy chair out to the left, the loud grinding noise expressing her displeasure.

Picking up the heavy, ornate fountain pen to sign her name, she felt his horrible chubby hand resting on her shoulder. She signed her name so quickly that the signature looked crooked and spidery. When she put the pen down, he squeezed her shoulder, not moving his hand until he had made a prolonged examination of the signature. Its removal was a relief to Derryn, but the feeling would be short-lived.

"Mrs Evans, one more thing. A new family will be moving into your cottage shortly. You need to move by Friday."

"Friday!" she exclaimed, "that is not even a week."

"Yes, but your husband's contract stated that…"

His fat finger tapped on the clause in question.

"Do not even consider asking me for rent this week," she said firmly, just managing not to lose her temper. "What you are suggesting is entirely unacceptable."

"The contract says seven days from the day of death, Mrs Evans."

"That makes in Monday week, Mr Griffiths, and not a day before."

The manager gave a patronising smile and a small shake of his fleshy round head.

"Your husband only had nine years' tenure, not ten, so I am afraid that means five days' notice, not seven."

He paused momentarily, enjoying watching Derryn's panic build.

"If you require a place to live for a short while, I have a room available in my house," Mr Griffiths could imagine long nights of passion, taking advantage of a downtrodden widow. "It would make me a happy man to have a woman in the house again."

"However precarious my situation might appear, Mr Griffiths, I do not ever envisage living in your house. You are lecherous and demeaning. Should you continue your lewd behaviour, I will report you to the union. Mark my words."

Mr Griffiths was aghast, he had not expected such a response at all, and moreover, she had delivered it in the queen's English. Derryn might be a girl from the valley's now, but that wasn't always the case.

8

THE TRIP TO THE GROCER'S STORE

Derryn had been up since six o'clock. She had got to bed early the night before and awoke refreshed. Becca was still out like a light. The precious stillness in the cottage was soothing after all the upheaval of late. She lit the fire and warmed some water which she relished pouring into a small tin bath placed next to the hearth. She undressed and squeezed herself into the tub. She was just small enough to fit in if she pulled her legs tightly towards her chest. The water was toasty, invigorating even, as it washed away some of her woes just as much as grime. The hearty glow from the flames fluttering in the hearth warmed her as she sipped at a sugary mug of tea.

She washed her hair and body and eventually climbed out of the bath, the water temperature now feeling distinctly chilly. *I don't want this wretched cough getting any worse.* She dried herself off then cleaned her teeth with inky-black charcoal, swished and rinsed her mouth with the last of the warm water in the kettle and then chewed some fresh mint that she had grown in an old tin kept on the window sill. She dressed warmly, then sat in front of the fire to dry her long hair. Laying it over the front of her shoulder, it almost reached her lap.

It was at snatched moments like this when her world quietened, and she had time to think. Instead of a moment of respite, she now felt utter sadness. She grieved not for Tiny, but for herself and the whole dismal sorry world she lived in, a world that was about to get much worse when she would be forced to flee the family cottage. The beauty of the valley was tainted by horrible people like Mr Griffiths, and the mob, eager to banish poor Ludnow Gravis, the outcast from the village. His only crime in Derryn's eyes was offering solace to the bereaved in their hour of need. *Why is that a reason for such cruel persecution?*

The winter sun was low in the sky, and the wind was biting cold. It was the first time in weeks that she was able to see the sky. It was an icy cerulean blue, even though the richness faded with the faintest thin layer of white cloud, making the low, pale yellow glow seem even colder.

Time was marching on, and Derryn returned to the real world, starting with getting Becca up, breakfasted, dressed and ready for the day's errands ahead.

The mother and daughter made their way to the village, battling the cold wind that had won its struggle with the chimneys for once to take control of the valley's air. Although the blustery gales threatened to knock the frail or unwary off their feet, there were still people out and about taking care of their business. The haze from the colliery would soon dull the air again. For now, the buildings looked cheerful bathed in a hint of sunshine, Derryn made her way to the grocers. From there she would stop in at the bakery for a fresh loaf, and finally, the dairy for the smallest portion of butter and cheese they sold. Mr Jenkin's grocery store had become the hub of the village, perhaps even more than the church or pub. Its popularity meant the old couple knew about everything about everybody else's business, often thanks to eavesdropping on the tittle-tattle of the visiting village gossips. They didn't see it as nosiness, though, but rather a genuine way to show empathy and kindness towards their customers. Look after your customers, and they'll look after you was the Jenkin's motto.

"Hello, Mrs Jenkins," greeted Derryn.

"Oh. Hello, lass. And how are you then? Life has been hard on you this last while, so I've heard. You poor poppet."

"Yes, Mrs Jenkins," she confirmed. Moved by the kindness of the old woman, she felt tearful.

"Now, will you look at Becca, Harold. Isn't she as pretty as a picture in her bonnet and coat?"

Harold Jenkins was more concerned about the child's arms swinging wildly by some neatly stacked glass jars on a display table near the window.

Years of marriage had trained Mr Jenkins as well as a prized gun dog. He was now primed and ready to react to the sound of his wife's orders. These days he agreed with her the moment he heard the sound of his name, before waiting to find out what the request was.

Myfanwy Jenkins was a portly, cheerful woman with a head full of black hair intermingled with a fair few greys. Her dark brown eyes had thick black lashes. Her flushed cheeks were apple red. Always wearing a brightly coloured dress to work, she was a welcoming sight. It was impossible to feel melancholic in her company. She always had a joke or two up her sleeve to bring a smile to the glummest of faces.

Kindness radiated from the woman. If you looked particularly upset that day, she would swoop you into her little office, make you a strong cup of tea and mind all your business. She did it all with such sincerity that folks in the village didn't mind telling her everything. Once she had heard the forlorn person's news, she would offer her wisdom and then send them off with a box of homemade cakes. She never gossiped. Ever. No word of the troubles shared with her would ever reach another's ears. Secrets were safe with her. The villagers said she was more effective at calming an aching heart than Reverend Hughes.

"Mrs Jenkins, I need to be out of the cottage by Friday, and I need a room for Becca and me," she explained with desperation in her voice.

"Aw lass, that horrid Griffiths man has all but turfed you on the street now, has he? What with your Tiny saving those other men of his and the poor man barely in the ground, it's all wrong. I know it's not much Derryn, but perhaps you can take some comfort in knowing that it's not your fault. There really is nothing you could have done to fight the top brass at that mine. They have cast out so many widows at the drop of a hat that it's a disgrace. Let me make us a brew, and you can tell me all about it."

Before she could reply, the young mother and her daughter were rounded up and corralled into the tiny back office.

Derryn sank into a squishy but threadbare reading chair, the one reserved by the Jenkin's for visitors in need of solace. Once settled, she firmly slapped her lap with her hands to warn Becca it was time to stop spinning around like a whirly-gig and sit still on her knee. Becca obeyed for what felt like the first time in quite a while.

"I understand they need the place for a new family, Mrs Jenkins, but less than a week was terribly short notice. We only got five days from the date of the death, not seven cos Tiny had not been with 'em for ten years—only nine," lamented Derryn.

"Yes, me dear, indeed it is. Far too short a time to get yourself straight. What with a funeral to arrange and all that," agreed Mrs Jenkins.

She poured the tea out of a bold floral teapot and into matching cups. She put a piece of pound cake onto a plate and offered it to Becca. Becca had never seen a spread so beautiful, and it made her feel rather special. From the child's perspective, it was very grand.

"At least Mr Griffiths promised to settle the benevolent fund payment promptly, so I have the funds to pay someone to take on the rent. Twenty-four pounds will keep the wolf from the door."

"Well, that's something to cling onto, now isn't it, flower?"

Mrs Jenkins smiled reassuringly.

"Now, it just so happens I do know of a place coming up. The owner came in here and asked me to put some feelers out for a tenant. Might be just what you need, I reckon. It's a bit remote, but I don't think that will matter," explained Mrs Jenkins. "See how things just work out perfectly, even at the darkest of hours? It's here in the village, by little lane near the railway line. It's on Dr Pritchard's private land. He needs an occupant. The last tenant left all of a sudden without paying him. Perhaps we can go and have a look. It is a bit cheaper than other cottages, not because it is pokey, but because of the noisy locomotives passing by. The main thing is it's solid, cosy and dry. Just the job for you two."

"At this stage, anything will do, or we will be resorting to hiding in a shepherd's hut in another valley! I know this is not the best place in the world, but I can't imagine going back to Cardiff just yet, I first need to contact my father's lawyer."

"No, no, lass, I agree."

Derryn's last mouthful of tea went down the wrong way, and the attempt to quietly stifle the tickle in her throat quickly turned into an uncontrollable bark of a cough. Mrs Jenkins had to help the young woman replace her cup on the small table, her breathing was so laboured. Once her composure was recovered, Mrs Jenkins was keen to get going. She put her thick woollen jacket on, then gave the mother and daughter a commanding stare urging them to follow suit. Not wanting to waste any time she thrust their coats into their fumbling arms.

> "Come on now. Before someone else snaps it up. It'll be just your luck at the moment for that to happen."

With unbridled enthusiasm, she shooed them through the store and into the street. Despite her advancing years, Mrs Jenkins walked briskly ahead, the two hesitant youngsters awkwardly trotting behind her, not quite sure of where they were going or what they would find when they got there. Derryn wheezed with the exertion. Becca was as bouncy as ever.

In a short while, they were on a plot of land just by the railway line. The cottage appeared unlocked and Mrs Jenkins opened the door unashamed that she was looking about without the owner knowing.

"Oh, Dr Pritchard," sighed Mrs Jenkins "Now he is lush he is. When you see him, you will know why I say so."

With her breathing returning to normal, Derryn giggled at the remark.

The cottage was in good condition. It had two reasonable sized rooms, lit by the large south-facing windows. There were a couple of smaller windows on each side of the door that lit the entrance to what appeared to be a narrow kitchen and sitting area between the two larger rooms. There wasn't enough room or need for a coal shed on the land, but there was a large wooden box by the front door to securely store a couple of heavy sacks of coal close to where they would be needed.

The sturdy cast iron stove that stood in the far end was clean and modern. Because the cottage was situated on a patch of higher ground, there would be no danger of flooding. The whitewashed ceiling showed no sign of a leaking roof. There was a large water tank, and the privy was close. Out at the back was a washing line swaying in the wind. It was more comfortable and maintained than the miners' cottage, and Derryn couldn't believe her luck. Being that little bit further away from the pit head and the heart of the village, the choking smoke and coal dust would be lessened too.

"Now, Dr Pritchard is a busy man, and he has asked for Harold and I to manage collecting the rent—"

"—I'll take it!" Derryn interjected.

"But you don't even know how much it is, yet!" giggled Myfanwy.

"I don't care. Besides, you would never have told me about it if I couldn't afford it."

"You know me too well, young Derryn. Good, lass, I'll get it all sorted for you, and you can just give me the money, It's two and six a week. You can pay the first instalment on the day you move in."

"Oh, Mrs Jenkins, thank you so much. I have been so downhearted of late. I feel so much better now. If it's agreeable with you—Dr Pritchard—I'd like to pay you a few months in advance. It'll give me some peace of mind about the future."

Derryn's joyous step forward quickly became a terrible step back when she called out for Becca saying it was time to leave only to find there was no response. Her daughter did have a wayward temperament, but she never ran off. The anxious parent hunted high and low, running around the perimeter, looking into the bushes and hedgerows, her chesty cough hindering her pace.

"Come here, now, Becca. This is not funny!"

Mrs Jenkins joined the search, calling out her name, looking everywhere. For several minutes they hunted for the girl, but to no avail.

"What's that scuttling noise?" asked Derryn.

"What noise?"

"Shhh!"

Derryn turned her head to the noise and ran, flinging open the doors to a tiny coal cupboard. Inside was the girl, her hands and face blackened, grinning out at them. She was quickly yanked out and reprimanded by her fraught mother, before being hugged with relief.

Mrs Jenkins wrote a note to advise Doctor Pritchard the place was taken. She said she would pop round to see Edward Purvis with it later and get it dropped off at the doctor's residence.

They walked back to the village slowly, an exhausted Derryn holding onto Becca to keep her close. All the dashing around today had taken it out of the widowed woman. Finally, however, she felt her luck seemed to be changing.

"Thanks again, Myfanwy."

"It's a pleasure lass. Before you head off back to the row, let's go via the shop. I have some cakes I want to send you off with."

Derryn had a sense of hope once more. The excitement of moving out of the blackened row of miners' cottages was building by the second. She would not miss the coal dust saturating the air, but she would miss her friends. *It will be a wrench leaving the home I shared with Tiny—Becca's birthplace too. Still, it's a fresh start.* She began to imagine the small cottage kitted out with her treasured possessions and even went as far as to consider putting up a small curtain at each window.

The rest of the day she spent preparing for the imminent relocation, George Watkins had offered her the use of her sons for the move, and she had accepted on the spot. Bronwyn came to lend a hand.

"Are you still going to visit me, Bronnie?" asked Derryn.

"What kind of a question is that?" chided Bronwyn, "It's not like you are moving to London, is it?"

Derryn laughed.

"If you be up the hill and around the corner then, why would I not?"

"Well, I'll not be in the row anymore, and you know how busy the kids keep you an' all."

"It will be like a breath of fresh air over there. Of course, I will visit, you are going to see me almost every day, you are. If I can sneak off, I will," Bronwyn consoled her.

"And this Dr Pritchard," she asked, "do you know anything about him?"

"Not really, only the regular gossip going around the village. He's not married and a rather eligible bachelor, so they say."

She winked at Derryn.

"Tiny's barely cold in the ground," she snapped, becoming teary-eyed again, "so don't even joke, Bronwyn."

"Yeah, you're right, I shouldna pulled your leg."

"I don't know what's going on anymore, Bronwyn. There has been so much happening recently. I've had no time to think. Apart from a bath this morning. At least I think it was this morning—"

Derryn went quiet and picked at the black lace cuffs on her dress.

"Aw lass, just come here if you feel blue.
We'll look after you, do you hear?"

9

THE MOVE TO THE NEW COTTAGE

Derryn and Becca made their way back to their old cottage. It was five o'clock and already dark that Thursday afternoon. The foul wind blew frozen air into their faces, stinging their cheeks once more. They both raised their scarves until the wool almost met their eyes. The cottage was warm as they entered thanks to Derryn leaving the cinders burning. She stoked the fire, sliced some bread, ham and cheese, then she and Becca sat together and ate in front of the fire.

"Ma, we are closer to the big school when we move. Did you know that?"

"I'd been so busy getting us moved, I didn't even think of it," laughed Derryn, amazed at the little girl's power of observation.

"Yes, I can walk to school, Ma," she added. "I wonder when I can start? Where are you going to work, Ma?"

Becca in full interrogation mode exhausted Derryn even further.

She hadn't given thought to any of the girl's interrogations, but at least there was a little bit of money which would give her time to find a job. She was considering a position at the colliery cleaning coal. *Any pit-brow lass work will do.* She vowed to broach the subject with Mr Griffiths when she saw him again.

"Ma, is my Da ever coming back?"

"No, Rebecca," she snapped. "He won't be coming back. Ever. I've told you. Now, hush!"

It was as if she was answering more for herself than Becca. For the first time since Tiny's funeral, Derryn grasped the finality of her husband's death. It was easy to fill the time dealing with the practicalities of bereavement. There were jobs to be done, loose ends to be addressed. Duty guided the mind. Until now, she may have fooled herself that he was at work or the pub, but it was only now that, finally, she admitted they would never see him again, and incredible loss overtook her.

As eight o'clock approached, she picked up Becca and put her into bed, then she went back to the rocking chair, and the sadness overwhelmed her. She looked into the fire. All she could do was feel the pain and a sense of absolute isolation, a void so deep, dark and threatening that she began sinking into hopelessness. Exhausted, she fell asleep in front of the fire and woke up cold in the early hours of the morning. She went into the bedroom and climbed under the blankets. Gently, she put her arm around Becca. The child was warm and comforting. She tried to fall asleep, but her mind couldn't rest. It whirred and crunched, trying to work out what she should do next to support them.

George Watkins arrived with his empty cart early on the Friday morning at seven with his two sons in tow. The sun would not rise for quite some time yet.

"Dr Pritchard is a fine man, Derryn. He has a heart of gold. Helped a lot of people in the village. You'll be grand over there," said George to reassure her.

The boys set to work collecting her belongs and carefully strapping them down to the cart.

"Yes, I have heard many people say good things about him," answered Derryn, with a smile thinking about Mrs Jenkin's comment on his good looks.

By sunrise, Derryn's old cottage was utterly bare.

George knew it would be a wrench leaving the old family home. When the time came, he jollied Derryn along with a few words, urging her to join the lads outside before the weather turned nasty. She closed the door and turned the key then asked George to drop it off at the colliery office for her, which he gladly obliged.

Up ahead, Becca was running beside the lads and talking their ears off. For the little girl, the move to the new cottage was a huge adventure and being closer to Miss Bevan's school increased her excitement all the more.

"Da,'" shouted Mikey Watkins. "Where to is it from here, Da?'"

"Just up behind the station master's house, Mikey, around the corner. You go on ahead, I'll be there in a minute."

George and a wheezing Derryn followed at a slower pace, while the impatient youngsters raced up the hill pushing the cart with great gusto.

"Perhaps Dr Pritchard can get you something for that cough, Derryn."

The breathless woman nodded.

The small village was beginning to wake up as the cart continued to trundle onwards to its destination. The tiny bakery had its lights on and the smell of freshly baked bread laced the air. The grocery store and post office were opening their doors. The owners waved and greeted as they passed the shops, and Derryn found it uplifting seeing the welcoming faces.

"You going to be happy here, lass. It'll be different to being stuck out near the colliery. There will be a lot of company for you here," said George, "And if you're ever not happy, you just come to talk to me, like," he said reassuringly, knowing that some of the locals were still smarting over her request for the sin-eater to pay a visit to Tiny.

As George was speaking, Derryn was looking about and watching the storekeepers preparing their shops. There was already a man standing outside the bank waiting for it to open. As they got closer, Derryn recognised the hat and coat.

"My word, Derryn. That's Ludnow Gravis. He seldom comes into town, and if he does, he usually does his errands at the break of day to avoid seeing people."

"Morning, Ludnow," greeted George as they got closer.

Ludnow doffed his hat. It was the first time Derryn could see him properly. Her gaze fell upon an incredibly handsome man, blessed with bright blue eyes and the start of a slight smile that promised to become beautiful.

"How are you fettling, lad?" asked George without stopping to talk.

"Well, Sir, thank you."

"Good day, Mrs Evans," Ludnow greeted Derryn shyly.

Derryn smiled at him. For some unknown reason, she liked the mysterious stranger.

"Might see you in a bit then, Mr Gravis. Stay well," said George.

"Thank you, but I am off now. I've done what I needed to."

He nodded at Derryn, and moments later, he was gone. She looked at his wagon as it travelled down the lane and had a strange feeling of loss as she watched him go.

When Derryn and George caught up with the boys, they were busying themselves unloading the belongings before it rained. Later, after several chaotic trips through the narrow front door with her bulky furniture, resulting in several bruises on the boy's knuckles, Derry felt her new cottage was starting to feel a little less like an empty shell and a little more like home.

10

THE SCOURGE OF EFA BROWN

Mrs Jenkins had ensured that the cottage was spotless. There was a thoughtful gesture of a posy of primroses on the window sill, perched in a small glass jar. She'd also made sure there was a hearty fire going, and some water simmering in a jet-black kettle. Derryn immediately felt cheerful about discovering her kindness.

"George, can I make you and your boys a quick cuppa to say thank you?" asked Derryn.

"No, ta, Derryn. I gotta get that cart back. The lads are on the two o'clock shift, and they have things to do back home, but Francis and I will pop in next week sometime, if that is alright with you, like?"

"Of course, it is George. I shall see Mrs
Jenkins for some of that pound cake of hers.
Thank you for your help," she said with
sincerity.

What a lovely girl she is thought George as he walked
down the hill. He had grown very fond of her and
Tiny over the years. He hoped she could build the life
that she deserved. He knew Tiny's ways in his living
years. He was a bit of a show-off, a big mouth. Often,
he pushed his banter into the realm of bullying.
Secretly, George thought that the well-spoken girl
from the city was too good for her coarse colliery
husband.

Derryn's mind was on another issue. *How on earth
will I ever repay the Watkins family for their kindness?
They have done so much for me of late.*

"Bye then," chimed the chaps as they
trundled off, waving at her.

Derryn returned to the cottage and took a moment to
sit in her rocking chair, carefully positioned to give
the best view out of the window. She blessed them
all from afar for their kindness.

The next day, the sun had barely risen in the sky
when the first visitor arrived at her cottage. It had
been another sleepless night for Derryn, hugging
Becca as she pondered their future. Not wishing to
disturb the girl, later she chose to sit in her rocking

chair once more, taking in the restful view. When Derryn saw Efa Brown open the gate at the bottom of the garden, she had an urge to lock the door and pretend that she was not at home. After the debacle with the villagers, after Efa had been seen visiting last time with Ludnow, Derryn didn't want any more trouble.

She watched the old woman march up the muddy footpath, making no attempt to stop her dress dragging along the sodden ground. Her grey hair was scraped back, only just visible under her black bonnet. Where it wasn't muddy, her dress was also jet black. She looked like a walking bad omen. The skin on her thin face sagged around her jowls, and a criss-cross of deep lines covered her face. Her mouth was slightly pursed, giving her a stern, disapproving expression. She was leaning forward, walking with determination like somebody on their way to deliver an urgent message.

There was a loud knock at the door, and reluctantly Derryn opened up and forced a smile.

"Hello, Derryn. Can I come in?"

Not waiting for the invitation, she pushed her way into the cottage regardless.

"Morning, Efa. This is rather—unexpected. What brings you here so early?"

"I've come to see how you're faring child and ask if I can do anything to help you? I know these early days can be so hard for a widow."

"Thank you for your interest, Efa. To be honest, my feet haven't touched the ground yet, what with having to move in such haste, but I know that we will be happy. It has a couple rooms which is plenty big enough for the two of us. It has a feel of the country about it—"

Efa Brown cut Derryn short with an interruption.

"Are you making tea lass? A cuppa would be welcome."

"Of course," answered Derryn good-naturedly, but annoyed at Efa further imposition.

"Where is the girl then?" asked Efa Brown, looking around.

"Why she is under that bundle of bedclothes in her bedroom," laughed Derryn, "can't yer see the bump there?"

Becca popped out with a big smile.

"Hello, Mrs Brown," she said with glee.

Efa Brown nodded sternly as if annoyed by the triviality of the exchange. The small talk was slowing her progress of probing Derryn for all the latest news.

"Have you met Dr Pritchard yet?" she asked.

"No, not yet. I've only been here one night," Derryn answered with a hint of exasperation. *What's it got to do with you?*

Efa tutted and shook her head.

"I would have thought he would have interviewed you? Seeing as you're his new tenant."

"No. Mrs Jenkins arranged it for me. She was very kind to do it. Dr Pritchard trusted her judgement and chose to delegate finding a family for this place to her."

"Mmm, yes. Let me tell you something. Dr Pritchard is a fine man, and he has very high standards."

"Yes, I have heard good things about him."

"Well, he is very fussy, you see?"

"No, I don't see. How could I? I've never met him. What are you trying to say, Efa? For goodness sake, spit it out," Derryn prickled.

"Well, you know, I don't know what yer standards are lass, but he won't tolerate behaviour like in the row," She shook her head slowly from side to side. "No, he is not a man to tolerate shenanigans."

Derryn was finding it difficult to keep calm.

"Are you done with your tea—you haven't touched it?" she asked Efa.

"Do you want me to leave? I have only come to give you some friendly advice. Like when I took care of your affairs when yer husband died."

"Yes, you did Efa. But you overstepped the mark. You should have washed and wrapped the body and left it at that. It was the most terrible thing I have ever seen what you put that man through. It was shameful. And the uproar it caused in the community, well—"

"That man has the devil in him from way back. Don't ye go on telling me I blackened his soul."

Her voice was loud.

"The sins of your husband are probably some of the heaviest he has had to bargain for, your Tiny would be burning in the pits of hell if it was not for me!"

"Tiny's soul is not burning anywhere," Derryn said firmly.

"Are you sure about Tiny, are you?"

She looked at Derryn with an evil bitterness.

"You are so full of yourself, Derryn Evans.
Well, let me tell you something, me dearie.
He was an adulterer. Yes. The whole village
knew except you. Yes, Tiny was womanising
with the best of them. Usually just for a night,
but there was one woman who was with him
for much longer. Nice little thing too. Do you
remember all that overtime he did? Why he
seemed to get every shift going? Yes? Why do
you think everybody was so kind to you,
Derryn? They felt sorry for you and the
bairn. Do you still think he wouldn't be
burning in hell were it not for me?"

Derryn ignored the question and asked one of her
own.

"Who is she, this woman?" demanded
Derryn. "I want to know."

"A strumpet he met at The Dragon."

After delivering her bombshell, Efa stood up and
straightened her damp and muddy dress in an
attempt to showcase the sacrifice she had made to
come and visit. She shook her head from side to side
with an expression of superiority, leaving her cold
tea and prepared to leave a stunned Derryn behind.

"That's what you gets when you try to help somebody," the old woman muttered, before grunting as she heaved open the door.

Efa Brown flew down the path to the gate like a hurricane, leaving a trail of destruction and devastation in her wake.

The confused widow couldn't get to Bronwyn's cottage fast enough. She dragged Becca through the village and down the hill to the row. By the time she reached her friend's cottage, she was a sweaty rasping mess. With the side of her fists, she pummelled at the front door.

"Bronwyn! Open up, will you?"

Willy opened the door.

"Sorry, Derryn," he apologised. "Ma has taken me Da's lunch over to him. The silly fool forgot it because he left in a rush. Look, it's wet out there. Do you want to wait here? She'll be back soon enough."

"No, thank you, Willy," Derryn replied, "but watch Becca for me, won't you?"

"Yeah, alright," agreed the lad. "Is she allowed out with Annie? I know there's a game of hopscotch going on. She might enjoy that? There will be lots of other children to play with. Might take her mind off things?"

"Yes, fine," shouted Derryn over her
shoulder, "but she must stay in her raincoat,
Willy. Tell Annie, won't you."

The heartbroken widow was close to hysterical now. She desperately needed a chat with Bronwyn to unburden herself of Efa's dark news of the philandering. Her heart was racing with anxiety. Her mind was desperate to hear the truth. But perhaps her most pertinent question of all was: 'had Bronwyn known about this all along?' When Derryn reached the mine yard, she almost toppled over for lack of breath. Bronwyn had seen her rushing down the hill and ran over to her as she entered the colliery gate.

"What's the matter?" asked a concerned
Bronwyn.

"Did you know?" screamed Derryn.

"Know what?" asked Bronwyn.

"Did you know that my Tiny was seeing
another woman?"

Everybody in earshot and beyond turned to observe the lunatic widow who had run into the colliery yard behaving hysterically.

"Come, let's go home," cooed Bronwyn,
giving her husband's lunch to someone else
to pass on to him.

"I am asking you, and I want an answer now!" yelled Derryn.

"C'mon Derryn. Not here in the yard where these people can see you. Don't give them a show like."

"I don't care if the whole colliery hears me, it seems everybody knew anyway! Everybody! Why didn't you tell me, Bronwyn? You're supposed to be my friend. Why did yer not tell me?" She repeated.

"Because I didn't want to hurt you, Derryn."

She dropped her head in shame. She reached out to take Derryn's arm, but she shoved her away angrily.

Not wanting to fuel the village's gossiping tongues for months, Bronwyn started to walk up the hill to the row. Derryn followed her. She tried to run, but she was angry and sad and just too exhausted to keep up the pace. Derryn's chesty cough filled the air.

Bronwyn reached her house and went straight to the kitchen.

Derryn stormed in behind, glistening tears running down her puffy face, glad Becca had already gone with Annie. She didn't want to be seen in such a state and cause her to worry.

"Tell me everything you know, Bronwyn
Brown. Everything! Who was she? Where did
they meet? When did they meet? I want to
know right now."

A drained Derryn lost a lot of her physical feistiness.
She let Bronwyn gently guide her into her armchair.
The widow sank down and began to cry.

Bronwyn poured some tea for her guest and passed
it with a compassionate smile. Then she sat on a
rickety wooden chair alongside. She put her arms
around her friend and hugged her. Derryn was about
five years younger than Bronwyn, and she had
always been like a little sister to her.

"Derryn. My Edwyn was up by The Dragon
pub one Saturday night. He saw Tiny come in
and then he and a woman left at the same
time. Eddy didn't think anything of it,
thought he was just helping the lass get
home safely, what with him seeming so
happy at home. But the next Wednesday—he
saw it happen again."

Derryn stared ahead of her, not believing what she
was hearing.

"Of course, my husband isn't much of a
talker, but then he heard the banter at work.
The blokes seemed to have cottoned on to
the story. You know what them lot are like.

Thick as thieves. They never dob their mates in with the wife. He only told me because he knew how close we are. It weighed down heavily on his conscience, you see. He didn't know what to do. Neither did I. I didn't want to break your heart over a silly fling. I knew you were a good wife for him. Why trouble you with something that meant nothing to Tiny? I thought it would blow over soon enough once he got it out of his system, and he would settle back down again."

"But it didn't end, did it?"

"No, Derryn."

"What's her name?"

"Connie Jones. She lives at the Golden Bell Hotel," answered Bronwyn, ashamed that she had not told her friend before.

"That's a brothel, is it not?"

 "Yes."

"Was she at the funeral, Bron?"

"Yes. At the back. Keeping a low profile, I suppose."

Derryn was filled with an emotion she couldn't fathom. It wasn't akin to the suffering bereavement brings. It was a toxic mixture of fury and disappointment. It was hard for her to work out which was more potent. The man she believed was a true and loving husband had betrayed her.

She reached forward and put her mug on the table, then slumped further still, resting her folded arms on the table, exhausted. She buried her head in the crook of her right arm closed her eyes for just a moment, desperately wanting to shut the world out and have a little privacy for her teary face.

11

THE CART THAT
CAME UP THE HILL

Bronwyn let Derryn fall asleep at the table. She looked so tired that Bronwyn wasn't sure if her friend had the energy to climb the hill back to her cottage. *The rest will do her good, poor thing.*

Willy was chatting to his pals a few houses down the row when he saw a horse and cart in the distance. It had turned into the road west of the colliery. It was followed by a string of colliers and children as if they were welcoming a travelling circus to town. The cart moved slowly up the hill. As it got closer, Willy saw two colliers sitting on the back of the cart. The driver was a big man, hunched over against the cold with a hat pulled low over his face. There was no doubt for Willy that it was Ludnow Gravis. It was odd to see him out like that. Usually, he kept his distance from the miners, preferring to have even less to do with them than the rest of the villagers. Then he saw his little sister on the back of the cart accompanying him. It was most peculiar that she was travelling with three grown men. He saw that she was filthy from head to toe. He pointed at her as she approached and chuckled so hard his belly visibly shook. *Looks like she has fallen in the dirt good and proper, in her best dress and coat too. Ma will be furious. I'll be able to tease her for years about the telling off she's going to get!*

The wagon came closer still. By now, he could hear a very hoarse Annie trying to scream blue murder. A miner, also plastered with dirt, shuffled along on his hands and heels to the tail-end of the wagon. Quietly, he climbed off the back. The other man still on the cart carefully lifted up a small child and passed it down. Willy wasn't chuckling anymore. It was clear something was gravely wrong.

The child lay limp in the man's arms, with its one arm swinging without resistance and the head was tilted back. The mouth was wide open but loosely packed with earth. Thankfully, the eyes were protected, her eyelids closed. Willy looked beyond the miner. Annie was still hysterical. With his hands now free, the man on the wagon bundled Annie off. His thick arms clamped around her to stop her thrashing about. Willy Brown recognised the fellow as one of the overmen from the colliery. He ran towards the limp child. The moment he realised it was Becca, under all the dirt, he turned around and ran all the way back to his mother's house, and tore into the kitchen.

"Ma, Ma!" he yelled. "You have to come outside. Something terrible has happened."

"Shush! You'll wake her," whispered Bronwyn, nodding her head in Derryn's direction.

It was too late. The dozing widow suddenly sat bolt upright. She could see a man carrying her child up the short path. The scene was surreal. The grubby little head and tiny arms hung limply, flopping about with every step the man took. Instinctively, Derryn recognised it was her little Becca. She let out a pitiful howl that could be heard throughout the valley. Nobody would forget it for years.

"Oh, my baby," she screamed. "What has happened to you?"

George Watkins pushed through the crowd toward Derryn.

"I want my baby. Bring her here!" she screamed hysterically.

"I know lass. I know. We will get her. We will. Come with me."

Derryn grabbed the muddy child out of the man's arms, cradling her and trying to open her eyes.

"Come, Becca! Come, wake up."

She put her fingers into the child's mouth
and started digging out the mud, then she
shook her, "Wake up, Becca. Now! I am
talking to you. Woe betide you if this is one
of your games!"

Ludnow couldn't stand watching Derryn's suffering.
He climbed off the cart's driving seat and walked
toward her.

"Come on. You can breathe now. Come on.
Your ma's here. Wake up, little one."

His soothing voice was in sharp contrast to the
wailing of the mother. He couldn't stand the sound of
her sorrow. He had been their himself, and he could
feel her agony. To the shock of the bystanders, the
huge man put his arms around Derryn and Becca.
They had never seen this loner of a man interact with
any human. They stood agog, hushed by the
tenderness he displayed.

"She won't wake up, Mrs Evans, but we can
still take care of her. Come now. Let me take
you both home."

George tried to help Derryn onto the wagon, but she
wouldn't release her grip on Becca. They had to wait
until she was too fatigued to resist their help.
Eventually, she climbed up with the assistance of

Willy and George. Becca was laid out next to her, her head held steady and cushioned by a folded-up sack. The cart began its slow, creeping ascent up the hill to Dr Pritchard's cottage. As they made their way towards the heart of the village, as a mark of respect, the miners were still escorting poor Derryn. Bronwyn and George walked respectfully alongside, giving each other worried glances.

Derryn stared vacantly towards the sky as if receiving some sort of vision.

Ludnow Gravis steered the cart through the tiny High Street, his hat pulled low over his face. He felt it kept his vast bulk invisible to the villagers who, he assumed, would only have eyes for the mother and child. Shopkeepers came out onto the pavement. Mrs Jenkins rushed out and took up a position behind the cart as well. *Oh, Dear God. Why did the angel of death have to revisit poor Derryn?*

Ludnow felt the horror of the child's death. He couldn't decipher why God had chosen put him on that road, on that afternoon, knowing that it would break his heart. The rain began to pour down in torrents, and he turned and looked over his shoulder to check on his passengers. He could see Derryn talking to the child as though she could still hear her. He couldn't stand to watch them and turned around again.

When they reached the cottage, he beckoned Derryn to come towards him. His commanding presence made sure none of the other men stepped in to assist. Awkwardly, she shuffled along with the wagon not letting go of the child for a second. Finally, at the edge of the cart, Ludnow swept the two of them up in his arms and carried them towards the cottage. One of the other men dashed ahead and tried the door. Luckily, it was unlocked. Ludnow carried his precious cargo to Derryn's bed, the softest place he could think of. He lay them down gently and then fled. He had to get away from the place. He geed up his horse with a sharp whistle, a dig of his heels and a crack of the long leather reins, then turned his wagon back along the small lane to head home as fast as he could.

As soon as Ludnow had gone, Derryn quickly got up and kicked her bedroom door shut, tired of being the focus of everyone's attention. The grief-stricken mother tucked her dead child under the eiderdown. She lay alongside her and clutched onto her little frame like she always did. Lots of people hovered outside, peering in through the windows. Some were driven by nosiness, but most folks genuinely cared about the young woman. After fifteen minutes, Bronwyn could stand it no longer and went in to take control of the situation. Eventually, after a lengthy discussion through the closed bedroom door, she managed to convince Derryn to put the child onto the table.

"Come, Derryn," said Bronwyn gently. "Let us
lay her down here and make her clean and
fresh smelling. Then you can spend time with
her again." She tried to give Derryn the chore
of boiling water to distract her, but it didn't
work. Eventually, she allowed Derryn to
stand next to the child and hold the little
white hand with the tiniest fingers.

Edwyn arrived at the cottage after his shift. He gave
a quiet knock, then peered through one of the
entrance windows. When he saw Becca, a look of
shock crossed his face. He could barely believe what
he was seeing. Bronwyn leapt up and opened the
door.

"Oh, Bronwyn," he whispered, "I so hoped
this wasn't true."

He looked at Derryn who began to sob once more.
She tried to wipe the tears from her eyes. Her nose
was running, making her sleeves damper still.

"Oh, this is so cruel," said Edwyn. He put his
hand on her forearm and squeezed it, trying
to calm her, but she wouldn't stop bawling.

Before Bronwyn could close the door, there was a
rustle in the crowd, and three women appeared at
the steps. They were black from head to toe, like a
vision of death itself. The umbrellas they carried
looked like sickles.

"We are here to help," said a voice.

Bronwyn and Derryn looked at each other with dread. It was the voice of Efa Brown.

The feisty woman pushed her way through inside and started removing her coat.

"Move yourself, Bronwyn," she ordered. "I'll take over from here."

"No, thank you," said Bronwyn commandingly, keen to avoid the trouble that was bound to accompany Efa's assistance. "We will be fine."

"Let the mother speak for herself," sneered Efa looking at Derryn.

"Leave her alone, Efa. It's no time to torment her," piped up Bronwyn in her friend's defence.

"This is what you get for not heeding me warning from before. I want to tell you something, and you better listen up good. This is for not taking matters of the soul seriously," advised Efa Brown so loudly that everybody outside the cottage could hear her. "I knew something would happen. I knew it. You have only yourself to blame. I tried to warn you of your husband's wicked ways. The sins of the father are being visited upon the child."

Nobody could have predicted what happened next. Derryn behaved like a wild cat. She launched herself across the cottage, going straight for Efa's throat. The violent lurch knocked the old woman over. Efa slid downside of the door frame. She landed in a tumbled heap on the floor, with her attacker flailing on top of her. Derryn put her hands around Efa's throat and began to choke her. Efa's eyes bulged, and her breath rasped. Bronwyn and Edwyn tried to pull her off, but the grieving assailant had the strength of a lion. The more they pulled, the tighter her grip became around the woman's neck.

To the onlookers, not looking through Derryn's lens now clouded by angry red mist, Efa clearly couldn't breathe. Her lips were trembling and blue. Her eyes were becoming vacant, and her mouth was wide open, trying to find air. Derryn could smell her acrid stinking breath and see into her mouth with all its missing teeth. Efa's feet were kicking uncontrollably. Bronwyn knew that if she didn't get Derryn off the woman, her friend would hang for murder. Bronwyn made a fist and hit the hysterical woman as hard as she could. The blow dazed Derryn and lights flashed before her eyes. At last, she loosened her grip and Ed took the opportunity to restrain her.

Mrs Jenkins and George Watkins ran forward.

"George, I'm going to fetch Dr Pritchard. She needs sedation," said Fran Watkins.

"Yes, Franny. Make sure you run, now, you hear me!"

Mrs Jenkins took over the restraint of Derryn, still berserk with rage. With the help of her fellow crones, Efa tried and failed to struggle to her feet. Her ancient body would not allow her to move fast, and her cohorts were too frail to lift her. Eventually, with reluctance, George helped her up. Efa had purple finger-shaped bruises around her shrivelled neck. All her former bravado and bluster had evaporated.

She started to cough, it was wracking, and her old fragile ribs ached in the cold. Her friends took her by the arm and led her silently down the path, limping and struggling to stand. It was only when Efa got halfway down the road back to the village that she was brave enough to attempt to curse Derryn. However, after her ordeal, she couldn't speak properly. Her voice was hoarsely leaving her unable to utter a word. The old witch's reign of terror was over, she would never interfere with the living or the dead again.

Dr Pritchard pushed his way through the spectators. He politely knocked on the cottage door even though it was open.

"Thank you for coming, Doctor," Bronwyn whispered to the handsome man on the doorstep.

"What has happened?" he asked, seeing the limp child.

"There was a terrible accident," answered Edwyn. "Somehow the children ended up playing on the big slag heap. She was swallowed up by it as if she were in quicksand. A couple of the men were taking tea above ground, and they heard the screaming. They went to fetch her out. Risked their lives doing it, like, but they couldna save both girls, just the one. It was too late for poor Becca here."

It was the first time Derryn heard the cause of Becca's death, and she began to wail all over again.

"Oh no! I should never have left her! My baby!"

She thrashed about and screamed as a protective Bronwyn fought to hold her still.

Dr Pritchard took out a large steel syringe and a vial of liquid from his doctor's bag. He drew morphine, and when the device was full, he smoothly injected it into Derryn's arm. She was so distraught that she didn't even feel the pain of the thick needle now embedded in her flesh. All she knew what that in moments, she became very sleepy and escaped into peaceful nothingness.

"I'll be back a bit later to check up on her. I suggest the crowd outside get a move on home. There is nothing they can do now. It's dark and cold, but the mourners will always tend to stay of course, until you grant them permission to leave," advised Dr Pritchard.

Ed nodded, "I'll see to that, doc?"

"Who is staying with her?" asked Dr Pritchard.

"George, Franny, Mrs Jenkins and us," replied Bronwyn, looking at Edwyn.

They all nodded.

"Good. Perhaps you can have the child collected by the undertaker before Mrs Evans wakes up. It will be better to see the child cleaned and comfortable. I am sure the undertaker will assist. You can always return the coffin here if Derryn wants to hold a wake. I think it may help her state of mind, but we can discuss that later. It is a pity this. A terrible pity. When are they going to fence off that godforsaken slag heap? It has been a contentious issue between the mine and the village for years. The owners have been lucky to escape with near misses to date. The union needs to get involved before it steals another young life."

Since death never kept to formal business hours, the undertaker lived above the premises. Dr Pritchard returned just before midnight. Derryn had begun to toss and mumble in her sleep.

"I am going to give her another injection," he told Bronwyn. "She must be exhausted with two deaths so close together, and the stress of moving her. It's best if she sleeps through until at least midday tomorrow and then we will see what we do after that. I had high hopes of this being a happy homestead for my tenants. It seems that was not to be."

Even though it was customary for mourners to keep vigil all night, Bronwyn and Ed sent the Watkins couple home. "You gave them so much help when they moved here. Let us step in to help now. You go and get some sleep, please, Franny. Could you bring us some food in the morning? Derryn will be awake then, and we will need all your help."

Mrs Jenkins and Bronwyn went about cleaning the cottage entrance, sweeping up the mud and coal dust. Finally, with the floor spick and span once more, there was peace. The women made some heart-warming tea for the three of them, and they sat down next to the fire.

Ed went over to Bronwyn and perched on the arm of the wooden chair. He took her into his arms, seeing the tell-tale signs she was about to break down and cry.

"How did this all come about, Bronwyn? What was she doing back up at Miners Row when she had this place?" he asked.

"She found out about Tiny's affair and came to find me at the mine when I brought your lunch over. The kids told Willy they were going off to play hopscotch. Turns out they wanted to roll down the steep side of that massive slag heap instead. The next thing, Ludnow Gravis of all people was driving a cart up towards the row, and little Becca was flopped out in the back of it, stone dead. Poor little mite's mouth was chock full of coal clinker as she fought for breath before she went under."

Edwyn shook his head as he explained.

"If I had not forgotten my lunch, this wouldn't have happened. You could have both kept an eye on them as they played outside, Bron. If the children hadn't escaped proper supervision, this wouldn't have happened. How is poor Derryn ever going to survive this? Little Becca was her life. And she's discovered that Tiny, her soulmate, was, in fact, a lecherous cad. When she visits, she'll see our family all fit and healthy, living the life of Riley. That will make her loss hurt all the more."

"You can't blame yourself, Edwyn. She wouldn't want us putting our lives on hold, tip-toeing around her. Stop it. 'Tis bad enough Derryn is hysterical, without you getting all agitated. We need to keep our wits about us. No wallowing. No self-pity. Do you hear me? We need to be strong for her."

He nodded, but he was struggling to convince himself that she was correct.

12

THE DEMONIC VISION

Rebecca Evan's funeral service was held at the church on the bleak hilltop. The little girl was buried next to her father in the cemetery bordering the solid grey stone building. The miners who were off-shift attended, bringing their children with them. They had good reason to. Firstly, a lot of them knew Becca and wanted to pay their respects. Secondly, it would terrify their children away from the murderous slag heaps. With every step that she took behind the little white coffin, Derryn thought she was going to go mad. The grief surpassed anything that she had ever experienced with the death of her parents or her husband.

The sky was clear and crisp. It was the finest day they had seen in a long time. Where she had felt distant and remote at Tiny's funeral, with Becca's, she thought she was in the dead centre of it. The choir set her nerves on edge, and she wished they would just shut up. The hymns dragged out the service. She wanted the whole business over with, tired of the sympathetic stares and endless silently mouthed condolences from the congregation. The minister's words brought no comfort if anything they jarred. He made no effort, trotting out the same old sermon,. He told them faith and love conquered all and that God knew best for each and every one of his flock. Derryn was quite sure that God was not doing the best for her.

Every time she looked at coffin, she could imagine Becca lying in it wearing her favourite white dress. If she thought the church was difficult, the grave was a nightmare. As the little white coffin was lowered into the earth, she became hysterical again, imagining that once earth had swallowed her up, something awful would happen. It was clear God had forsaken her and that her life was dancing to the beat of the devil's drum. She imagined dark underworld demons in a feeding frenzy, breaking a hole in the wall, their bony skeletal hands grasping at the delicate fresh pale flesh within. In a trance brought on by the melancholy, Derryn tried to throw herself into the grave as the first few mourners' handfuls of earth splattered onto the lid. George and Edwyn didn't doubt that had not pulled her back, she would likely have ended up at the bottom of the pit with a broken neck. The doctor had given them a potion for her to take if the hysteria returned at the service. It was swiftly administered by George, who took her to one side to preserve her dignity. While Edwyn held her still, George held the tiny bottle to her lips and pinched her nostrils until she had to open her mouth to breathe. In a flash, the full dose was dispensed. After a little spluttering from the shock, Derryn's face took on a relaxed frozen expression. However, her body still could walk.

After the service, Bronwyn mentioned that Derryn should never be left alone, not even for a moment. The Jenkin's offered to take the confused, grieving back to their own home above their grocery store. They explained there was a bit of space available if they moved the stock out of the spare room. They agreed to look after her until she was fit enough to go back to live on her own. Bronwyn dashed off after announcing she would pack a few essentials for Derryn. Mrs Jenkins slowly walked her into the village, then took her upstairs and put her to bed. She lit the fire and administered another dose of the medicine to make Derryn sleep.

"You will need to watch her, Mrs Jenkins," advised Bronwyn.

"I know, I know lass, don't you worry now, I won't leave her side."

Mrs Jenkins was as good as her word. Mr Jenkins stepped up to run the shop single-handedly. Thankfully, the villagers were very patient with the slow service, given the sombre circumstances.

When Derryn did come round, it was like she was stuck, with her asking the same questions over and over.

"Why has this happened, Mrs Jenkins? Why have I lost all the people I have loved? Is it as Efa Brown says, I am being punished for Tiny's sinfulness?"

"Let's have less of that talk, Missy. Efa Brown is evil," said Mrs Jenkins. "She has bought much ill for a lot of people. I am not a superstitious woman, but I know in my bones that bad follows her wherever she goes."

It would be a day or two yet of heavy sedation before Derryn would want to face reality again. When she did, she would sit and brood, going over the recent tragedies to befall her.

"I am sorry I am such a burden to you and Mr Jenkins."

"You're no such thing!" Mrs Jenkins would say reassuringly. "You stay as long as you like my girl. You are no trouble. I enjoy the company. After forty years under the same roof with Mr Jenkins, we've said most of what we want to say to each other. I even know what goes on in his head. These days, he's more like my twin than my husband," she said with a laugh.

But Derryn knew in her heart she couldn't stay too long. After a couple of days, it was time to leave, and even though Mrs Jenkins had been so kind, she still longed for her own humble home. Reluctantly, her nearest and dearest agreed it was safe for her to go back to the cottage.

On the day she left the Jenkin's, Bronwyn was trusted with the task to get safely to the cottage. The midday sun was cheerful, and the spring felt just around the corner. When they reached the cottage, she saw that a few wildflowers in the garden had begun to blossom. Where before she would have considered this a good omen, a promise of joyous things to come, the gloom that had enveloped her of late promptly snuffed out that optimism.

Bronwyn got a fire going and put the kettle on. Mrs Jenkins had sent a box full of groceries that one of the Watkins lads had delivered for her, and together they put things in the tall larder cupboard. Bronwyn made Derryn some cocoa, accompanied by a thick slice of bread and butter. The cottage warmed up quickly, especially with the bright sunlight flooding onto the floor.

Derryn looked around her. It was clear someone had been in during her absence. They had made sure that everything belonging to Tiny and Becca was skilfully packed out of sight.

"Thank you for taking care of me, Bronwyn, I could never have coped without your support—everyone's support."

"Oh, it's nothing. It's the least I could do after—"

She stopped herself, not wishing to remind her friend of her prior knowledge of Tiny's infidelity.

"We packed up Becca and Tiny's things. We thought it would be easier for you if they weren't on show. Would you like me to get Willy to come and collect them? Their things will be worth a bob or two down at the second-hand stall."

Derryn shook her head.

"No, I want to keep them for a while, please."

Bronwyn nodded, acknowledging she would have felt the same way. *Once you give those things away, you can never get them back.*

"Are you going to be alright on ye own, Derryn? Somebody will call in every day. It will be a bit of company for you. And I am sure they will help with the chores. I will pop in when Edwyn gets back."

She hugged her friend.

"I am around the corner, right?"

Derryn nodded. She had no desire to speak.

As Bronwyn let herself out, Derryn sat in her chair, pretending to start some needlework. As soon as her friend was out of sight, Derryn stood up and went to her bedroom. She peeled back the big eiderdown and climbed under it. She could still smell her child on the linen. She took one of the pillows, snuggling her nose deeply into it to get more of the smell. Clutching it tightly, she tried to fool her brain that it was Becca. Unlike the demonic graveside vision, her mind's eye was not going to be fooled by fantasy this time. It was clear the pillow was as cold and lifeless as her daughter was, and no amount of imagining would make it otherwise.

Derryn didn't leave her bed for days. When Francis or Mrs Jenkins came to check on her, they would find her asleep. Her hair was dirty and unkempt. Her immaculate appearance was replaced with one of neglect. She didn't change her clothes, preferring to stay in the same dress for days. Those who visited were never quite sure if she was asleep or was feigning sleep. The only sign of life was fresh nibbles on slices of bread and butter left on her bedside table. The level of the bottled spring water seemed to dip on occasions too. After a week Bronwyn put her foot down.

> "Now, I think we've had enough of this nonsense, don't you? It's time to be getting up and washing, my girl."

"I will tend to myself when you leave," argued Derryn.

"No, Derryn. Now. I know you are in a bad way, but you have to take some pride in yourself. What would Becca say if she saw you like this? All dishevelled. There's no way to put this, but you're in a right state."

Derryn didn't have the strength to fight and thought the sooner she complied, the sooner Bronwyn would go and she could get back in bed again.

Bronwyn lugged out the tin bath and filled it with water. She marched into the bedroom and flung back the eiderdown then roughly helped Derryn undress, indicating she had tired of her friend's self-pity, however understandable the cause of it.

Derryn's hour-glass figure was replaced by angular bones. She barely had the energy to walk, and Bronwyn had to help her. The dress and underwear smelled awful. Clearly, she had not felt like using the chamber pot at times. The fabric was unspeakably soiled. Bronwyn put the whole stinking bundle in the washtub outside, planning to deal with that unpleasant task later. She forcibly dragged a brush through Derryn's hair, the tangles regularly stopping the sweeping motion of her arm. When the bristles connected with the knots, she loathed seeing the force pulling her friend's head this way and that. She hated being so forceful, but if Derryn chose not to look after herself, then someone else would have to. And it needed to be made clear, that was only a temporary option. She pushed Derryn towards the bath.

"Get in. Here. You can wash your own hair."

Bronwyn thrust the soap into Derryn's hand. Slowly, Derryn lowered herself into the water. She was then given an enamel mug to ladle the water to rinse off the suds.

Once she saw Derryn doing as she was told, Bronwyn went off to make her a cheese sandwich. The surface of the cheese was going mouldy, having sat in the warm cupboard for far too long. Bronwyn trimmed off the worst of it and put what was left between two slices of questionable bread. Back in the bedroom, she ordered Derryn out of the water, then proceeded to dry her firmly with a scratchy rough towel that had seen better days. She lay a new dress and underwear on the bed and left her to put it on, mainly to test if Derryn had the will to do it herself without having to be yelled at.

Bronwyn left the room and heard the squeak of the bedframe as Derryn stood up, the creak of a corset being tightened, and the rustle of fabric tumbling down from head to toe. It was then she returned.

"Eat that. You look like a skeleton," she snapped, shoving the plate with the sandwich onto her lap.

By the time that her friend had finished bossing her about, Derryn had to concede that she felt better.

"What are you going to do with your days, Derryn?" asked Bronwyn. She knew that if her friend remained idle, it would not be good for her.

"I haven't thought about it."

"You still have time to look for something that might interest you. You have money for almost half a year. You don't have to settle for the first thing that comes along."

Derryn nodded, not wanting to discuss the subject. In fact, she didn't want to discuss anything.

Sensing that Derryn's temper was building, Bronwyn left her sat in the rocking chair, needlework in hand. The feeling of dread in the pit of her stomach grew as she looked back towards the cottage, fumbling absent-mindedly with the gate latch. She knew that it was going to be a long and arduous path for Derryn to walk back to any semblance of fulfilment. All she knew was that she would have to offer Derryn a lot of support for the foreseeable future. If she were honest, her good Samaritan act was as much for her benefit as her friend. It helped her atone for keeping schtum about Tiny's infidelity, and Becca's fatal accident, two trains of thought that quickly dragged her into a deep melancholy if she let them.

After all the effort Bronwyn had put in to help her, Derryn felt she shouldn't slope off back to bed at the first opportunity and persevered with the needlework. However, it seems she unpicked more than she sewed.

It was after sunset when she heard a horse at the gate followed by heavy footsteps coming up the path. She opened the door in anticipation of it being perhaps George or Edwyn. Who should greet her, but Ludnow Gravis walking toward the steps.

"Hello Derryn," he said.

"I am sorry to knock on your door this late," he said uncomfortably while he looked into her eyes.

She met his gaze and smiled, "No, bother," she said.

It was a pleasant surprise. For Derryn, Ludnow seemed to have a calming air about him. He never seemed to judge her or take over. He let her be herself, and for him, unlike a lot of other people in the village, that seemed to be enough.

"Please come in."

"Thank you," he said as he wiped his boots several times on the coir mat.

"What brings you out at this time?" She asked him shyly.

"I wanted to know how you are," he answered.

She smiled and nodded.

"Some days are better than others, but they are never good."

"I understand," he said softly.

"Tea, Mr Gravis? The kettle's hot."

"Go on then. And call me Ludnow."

She smiled and handed him his tea, and they drank it without saying a word. He was unimposing, and she felt comfortable in the silence.

"Derryn, you have to know. If you need my help, I am here for you."

He didn't qualify the statement. It was what it was.

"I didn't have time to thank you for bringing Becca and I back home," said Derryn, remembering his strong protective arms around her.

Ludnow stood up, looking perturbed by her comment.

"I better be going. I need to get back to the farm. It's late, and I still have a long list of jobs to do tonight."

"Thank you for thinking about me," said Derryn, hoping he might stay a little longer, but his mind was made up.

He nodded his head and smiled before striding back to his horse.

Derryn closed the door. The short conversation and company had made the night bearable. She hoped that she could see him again. There was something about him that made her feel safe, even if he was the village pariah.

13

THE VISIT BY DR PRITCHARD

The weather was warming up, but the smog of the chimneys still rose from the valley in pitch-black clouds. The pungent fumes spoiled the spring morning for Derryn, reminding her of Becca. From the cottage, she had a clear view of the neighbouring slag heap in the far distance, and it depressed her. She did her best to push it from her mind. *Dwelling on the past is not the answer.*

The idea of warming up in the hilltop sunshine was appealing, and Derryn made a steaming cup of cocoa with two lumps of sugar in it. She dragged the rocking chair outside, and she was almost at peace except for the thoughts of Becca, weighing heavily upon her soul. She would have loved to bound around the pretty little garden. She did what she could to put the blackness of bereavement to one side, and soaked up the golden light instead.

She heard a horse trotting and saw Dr Pritchard stop at the garden gate in his carriage. He strode up the pathway. It was the first time she saw the man properly. He was tall and fair. It was apparent that he was a man of means, impeccably dressed with the mannerisms of a prosperous gentleman.

"Good morning, Mrs Evans. I am glad to see you enjoying the fine weather."

He gave her a broad smile.

"Yes. It does so much to lift the mood," Derryn replied politely.

Although he didn't work outside for a living, she could see he had a toned physique. He was handsome and charming, a combination that would have delighted her in under other circumstances.

"You certainly look like the spring is returning to your step a little. Are you beginning to feel better?" he enquired.

"A little," she lied. "It's still early days, but nevertheless, here I am enjoying the fresh air. It's got rid of the terrible cough I used to have when I lived by the colliery."

She couldn't think of anything more to say.

"If you need anything, my home is just across the field. You are welcome at any time. I hate to think of you rattling around her on your own. I know it's not how you imagined life to be here."

"Thank you," answered Derryn in clipped tones.

Dr Pritchard realised that he was not going to get much more out of her that day.

"Well—I'll be off then. Goodbye, Mrs Evans."

"Goodbye," Derryn muttered.

She went back into the house looking for some more thread. She opened a cupboard, and her eyes fell upon Becca's boots. They were so small and perfect and barely used. They had been a special treat for her fifth birthday. Derryn began to cry. *Come on now. This is no use. Pick yourself up. You have to keep going.*

She decided the cottage needed a good spring clean and she began to prepare a bucket with water and a scrubbing brush. As she worked, she came across Becca's books in a box under her bed. They were books she had been so excited to read. *She never did make it the proper school.* Derryn spent an hour sitting next to the fire going through them, paying particular attention to her favourite pages denoted by the folded corner. Derryn had chastised her at the time for damaging the book. Now the folds were more valuable to her than gold. Next, she took out another box containing Becca's clothes and piled them around her as if making a nest. It was both comforting and heartbreaking at the same time. Eventually, she picked everything up, piled it onto the bed and began to clean. Once every flagstone was spotless, she looked at Becca's things but was not ready to deal with them just yet.

She went to the cupboard under the sink to take out a bar of carbolic soap. Next to it was a bottle of gin. Her fingers lingered around the stopper, then she pushed it aside. Edwyn and George must have had a drink together at some time when her nearest and dearest were taking it in turns for the bedside vigils.

She found the steel brush that she was looking for, and began scrubbing the stove, walls and floors. She went to back to the bed where she had piled Becca's clothes. She folded each item of clothing lovingly and packed it carefully into the trunk, smelling each piece as she did so. She closed the latches firmly, hoping it would help the clothes retain the smell of her daughter for longer.

She was glad she had not encountered Tiny's belongings yet, not that he had much apart from a few clothes and a clay pipe, not entirely sure how she would react.

It was late in the afternoon when she finally packed the cleaning paraphernalia back into the cupboard. Her eyes settled on the bottle of gin again. It was calling to her, but she ignored its pleas.

She lit the fire, cut herself a piece of bread and butter and sat down to eat. The effort she would have to make to brew tea for herself was an exhausting thought, so she gave up the idea. She sat on the rocker and watched the fire. The sunset was still early in the day and a long evening lay ahead of her. It would be a long dark void with nothing to fill it.

Wouldn't it be nice if Mr Gravis surprised me again? Startled by the thought that popped uninvited into her head, she put it out of her mind. *The devil makes work for idle hands and minds, Derryn. What are you thinking? He was just polite. A concerned neighbour, nothing more, nothing less.* Try as she might, she couldn't forget that he was attractive, rugged and capable. Secretly, she was drawn to those traits in a man. The discovery of Tiny's betrayal had left her bewildered. *How long should I mourn for a man who clearly had not a care in the world for his loyal wife?* She would not sleep as more intrusive thoughts, and dialogues filled her mind the moment her head touched the pillow. Clamping her eyes tightly shut in a temper did nothing. The thought of staying awake all night being tortured by her emotions tormented her. She was sure she didn't want to die in the literal sense. She felt she would lack the courage—but she did want to sleep forever and not wake up again.

Although the liquor in the cupboard could provide some temporary relief, she battled her conscience. She had seen too many folks' lives take a turn for the worse when the drinking escalated. So far in her life, she had resisted the temptation. It didn't seem to be the answer even if it was tempting.

Alas, with the voices in her head getting louder, she finally surrendered. Her pale hand lifted the gin bottle out of the darkness. Not really knowing how much to prescribe, a sizeable measure was carefully poured into a teacup to be on the safe side.

Derryn settled into the rocking chair next to the fire and prepared to take her first sip, then changed her mind and took a big gulp instead. *Kill or cure.*

At first, there was a bitter taste in her mouth then the burn of the liquor sinking down her gullet took her breath away. She almost threw the remainder of foul brew down the sink, but when the nagging voices returned, she decided to persevere. She gave the liquid the benefit of the doubt, thinking it might be the lesser of two evils.

She mixed in a little spring water and tried a few more sips which made her quest far more bearable. It wasn't long before she began to relax and within a short while, a wonderful sense of wellbeing came over her. It didn't remove her gnawing sorrow, but it did seem rather good at numbing the pain and stopping the chatter in her head. If she were honest, it began to feel good. She decided to have some more, just a half a cup this time, however. Then she planned to turn in for the night. Towards the end of the second dose, she was becoming accustomed to the taste. She decided to do one more small measure and, now she was more aware of what drinking liquor entailed. She finished another half a cupful, neat this time, without flinching. It certainly didn't taste any worse than some of the medicine she had endured earlier in her life. She put on her nightclothes, struggling to find the armholes. Try as she might, she couldn't smell Becca on any of the linen. She had resisted washing the sheets and resolved that it was sadly time to change them. Reaching under the bed, she dragged out the trunk and took one of Becca's dresses. She nuzzled her head into it until she was comfortable and then she fell into a deep, dream-free sleep and for the first time in days.

14

THE ARRIVAL OF SUMMER

The summer arrived, and it was an unusually warm year. The April showers had passed, leaving the streams running full. The village was a bustle of noise and cheer, and people could stop to chat without the threat of freezing or getting wet.

Derryn, however, had isolated herself more and more, over the last month or so, her days were empty, and the only trips she made into the village were for gin and food. She looked emaciated. Every night she drank until she collapsed. Her once curvy figure still all bones. Her skin was grey and pasty, and her eyes held no light. She was still neglectful of her appearance, despite Bronwyn's efforts to get her to buck her ideas up.

When people saw her, they would whisper to each other about how attractive she used to be, but alas no more. The golden hair was grubby and tangled, but it was her demeanour that had deteriorated the most. She was hard-nosed and unapproachable. She did her best to alienate all her friends.

Their concern deepening, the women closest to her called a meeting in the backroom of the Jenkin's grocery shop.

"I don't know what to do for her anymore," confessed Bronwyn to Francis Watkins. "If I go and visit her, the door is locked, and it takes ages for her to open up. She hardly talks, and she is filthy. If I even hint at helping her, she becomes aggressive. Getting that payment from the mine has turned into a curse. She has no reason to leave the cottage to work. It makes her choice to live like a hermit even easier. I am losing patience. I have very little time to myself, and I don't want to waste it on her if my efforts go by unappreciated. She seems determined to tumble into an abyss. I am losing the will to keep propping her up."

"I have to be honest, Bronwyn, I think she has taken to the bottle," replied Francis with concern in her voice. "I've heard talk that she regularly gets a big bottle of gin from Walter over at The Dragon."

"Yes, she is in and out of here like a ghost. I always ensure I put something cheerful into her box. To be fair, she does show some gratitude, but she doesn't stop to talk," said Myfanwy Jenkins.

They had all tried so hard to reach her, and eventually, after months of continuous rejection, her friends gave up and stopped calling on her.

Being alone had given Derryn a lot of time to sit and brood about Tiny's infidelity. Finding that out had been the catalyst to her life of eternal hardship. She had come to the point where the desire to see Connie Jones had become an obsession. The rancour in her mood built day by day. She knew that if Tiny had not already died, she was likely to have killed the philanderer with her bare hands. Derryn wanted to know the measure of this Connie woman. *Was she beautiful? Was she a good lover? Where had they met each other? What did she have that I couldn't give my husband? Where did they choose to lie together? And how many times? A few snatched occasions or hundreds?* The torrent of torturous unanswerable questions was both endless and excruciating.

It took all Derryn's courage to walk over to The Dragon to buy a bottle of gin. She knew all the regulars knew about Tiny's antics. The shame ran deep.

She had slept all day, and when she woke later on that Saturday night, she realised that she had almost run out of liquor. It didn't take her long to realise how hellish her day would be on Sunday without the comforting liquid to hand. By now, Derryn drank throughout the day and night. What had begun as an occasional comfort on the bad days was now a full-blown addiction. All her waking moments were spent obsessing about having enough to drink. It was the least unpleasant of her options to dwell upon.

"Mrs Evans! Good to see you, as always," lied Walter the barman, trained to always present a friendly face. There was very little to like about Derryn these days.

"Tell me now, what can I do for you? Usual, is it?"

"Yes—but, erm—can we make it two bottles?" she asked quietly. She decided to have a spare bottle to hand made good sense, should her foolishly let her supply run low again.

She carefully counted out the money and handed it over.

"I'll fetch it from the storeroom. I'll only be a minute. I will pour you one on the house, while you wait. You being such a good customer an' all."

"Oh, that's lush," whispered Derryn in quiet delight, as she saw the generous measure tumble into the glass. *I won't need to wait to get home for my first proper drink.*

She began to look around the pub. The old walls were propped with wide beams, and the bar counter was marked with scratches and dings made by the unruly miners. A black film of dust covered every available surface where the miners sat, it had stained the wood, and no amount of soap would wash it off. The wooden floor was covered with large stains, coal dust and boot marks. The pub was grubby after years of abuse, and the owner had given up trying to improve it. The tables and benches were sturdy enough to withstand wild parties and the wall behind the bar counter was filled with rows and rows of bottles to fuel the party-goers. Derryn had never imagined that there were so many different types of grog available.

Usually, she secretly collected her drink in the week from the hole-in-the-wall halfway down the alleyway to the pub's privies at the back of the premises. There had never been a need to go inside. Derryn preferred it that way, wrongly assuming that it helped to keep her addiction secret.

Feeling self-conscious, Derryn picked up her drink and moved to a far corner of the pub where she could observe the people and be invisible once more. There were several women in the pub. She recognised one or two of them from the row. They were as drunk and rowdy as the men, and mostly older women who had no children they had to care for. Their haggard faces might look tired, but they seemed to have plenty of energy to throw their heads back in laughter, grouped together like birds on a telegraph pole. Their clothes were old and patched. None of them had used a brush on their hair for some time, by the looks of it. She wondered if she resembled them to her onlookers when she went about her weekly errands the village, and correctly assumed yes.

Two men stood in the corner. One held a mouth organ and the other a fiddle. They were playing a song, but the harmonica player seemed to play whatever notes he felt like. Only the violin placed seemed to be able to hold a tune. A few women were doing a wild jig closer to the musicians, but their steps were out of time as they staggered about.

Derryn knew that this was where Tiny would come to meet his mistress. She found herself eyeing up the women one by one, trying to find one who she thought would be a match for her late husband, but none of them fitted the image of someone she believed Tiny would have chosen. None of them seemed to match her idea of Connie Jones. That, she concluded, was probably for the best.

A man emerged out of the chaos holding two glasses.

"Right! I don't want to lie to you lass, but what is a beauty like you doing alone in The Dragon?"

"I have never been here before. What I mean is, I am not a regular." she stammered.

The man laughed, his warm, flirtatious smile tugging at Derryn's heartstrings.

"I know that, or I would've noticed you before."

"I'm just waiting for Walter."

"Oh, are you his girl then?"

"No, I am buying something from him," she explained quietly, the shame stealing her voice.

"Well, let me buy you another round, like. Might as well make the most of a Saturday night if you've taken the trouble to come out."

"Tidy. Thank you."

She smiled at the fellow shyly. Derryn would usually have refused such a forward gesture. Still, she couldn't turn down the offer of more free booze.

As he approached the bar, the man saw Walter return with the two bottles of gin. Deducing the bottles must be for the woman since he would only need one if he had run out behind the bar, he asked Walter to store the bottles under the counter, and to pour a couple of drinks for him and 'the lady'.

One drink followed the next, and eventually, she began to enjoy the man's company and the crowd. Her depression faded, and her shame abated. The alcohol was doing its job. *Being around people didn't seem quite so terrible that night.*

Boldly she whispered in the man's ear.

"Do you know Connie Jones?" she asked.

"Yes. There she is at the bar. She's a beaut, alright. Pity, she charges—" The man's voice trailed off as he noticed his drinking partner take flight.

Derryn staggered to the bar doing her best to walk straight but finding it difficult.

She stood beside the woman, and she had to agree, Connie Jones was gorgeous. She had bright red hair, white skin and a perfectly pert and round bosom that she revealed in a daring, low-cut dress. She must have made to her own design since it was far more risqué than traditional Victorian fashions. The emerald green fabric offset her eyes and her hair. She stood smoking a cigarette in a long holder, held in place by a gloved hand. She was quite possibly the most elegant woman Derryn had seen in real life. Her lips were full, luscious and stained red, but it was her voluptuous curves that kept all the men's eyes glued to her. She clearly wanted to be a walking advert for her wares, and scandalised wagging tongues would make sure business was good.

"Are you Connie Jones?" asked Derryn.

"Yes," smiled the confident, older woman.

"My name isss Derryn Evansss!" she announced with misplaced over-confidence, aware of neither her slurring nor swaying.

Connie looked the dishevelled woman up and down without saying a word.

"You had an affair with my husband, Tiny, didn't you?"

"I have nothing to say to you, Mrs Evans. That was a long time ago," replied Connie in an angry raised tone.

"Not long enough, you harpy," shouted Derryn, louder still.

The music stopped, and the people gaped at the warring women.

"Pull yourself together," snapped Connie. "You are embarrassing yourself."

Derryn had months of pent up fury in her, and in her drunken state, she slapped her nemesis in the face.

Connie was far too experienced to react to an angry wife, or in this case, widow. She simply looked at Derryn with disdain. Derryn tried to attack her again, arms flailing, spittle flying from all the curse words, but she was stopped by two burly men.

"Calm down, lass. She isn't worth it."

Derryn started crying.

"My husband thought she was worth it," she shouted. "She is nothing but a common tart, and I thought she would be something special."

Of all the things that Derryn could have said, those were the worst words Connie thought she could utter. Connie had always been the centre of attention, and now it finally dawned on the whole bar that she was nothing more than a common, faded beauty, held together by corsetry, powder and paint. Horrified at the dramatic fall from her pedestal, Connie picked up her bag and walked toward the door, the deep red handprint across her beautiful face, issue by a ranting drunk was a humiliation that people would be talking about for weeks to come.

Derryn focused on her priorities again and looked over to Walter and asked for her bottles, then tucked them in her bag. She tottered back to the man, hoping her outburst would not cut the flow of the free drink.

She left the pub in the early hours of the morning, insisting that she could look after herself. She staggered to the door and managed to navigate her way down the steps out onto the lane. It was raining, and she was too drunk to dodge the puddles, walking straight through them drenching her boots and skirt.

The man watched her go. He decided she was quite something, strangely mesmerising. Not the typical barfly at all. He watched her turn down the lane that led to the station and vanish from view.

Derryn could see her cottage from where she was, in fact, she could see two cottages. She had never been this drunk in her life. Usually, she felt her drinking was medicinal, a convenient means to an end. Tonight, it had been different. It had greased the wheels as she mingled with the regulars and given her the courage to face Connie Jones—and win! Her head was spinning, and every step felt heavy. All she wanted to do was lie down on the side of the road and sleep. As she stumbled along the muddy lane holding her bag with her bottles of gin to her chest like they were the most precious treasure in the world, she almost lost her balance a few times. As her tired feet dragged through the ever-deepening potholes and puddles along the lane to her cottage, eventually, she stumbled and getting back on her feet proved to be too much of a struggle. Shattered, she slumped over at the side of the path, the cold, wet meadow grass sliding across her face. Then, she succumbed to sleep.

At dawn, Derryn woke up with a start. Even though she felt frightfully sick and her head seemed as if a wagon might have rolled over it in the night, she tried to stand. Her stomach rippled with an uncontrollable wretch, and an awful, bitter plume of vomit came racing up to her mouth. She put her mouth up to stop it, but it sprayed through her fingers, dripped down her sleeves and soaked into her hair. The smell almost brought about a repeat performance. She was more aware now but slumped back in the long grass to get over the nausea, not realising quite what she was laying in.

Still drunk and drifting between dozing and waking, she heard the rhythmic clip-clop of horse's hooves stop beside her. Hands pulled at her arms, forcing her to sit upright. Then some arms scooped her up like she was a child and cradled her. Drifting between consciousness and unconsciousness, she nestled against a warm chest. She must have passed out again because when she woke up again, she was in her bed and the bedclothes were pulled up to her chin. Beside her lay a bag with the two untouched bottles of gin within, not that she was in a fit state to notice.

Derryn felt as if a train had hit her. She tried to sit up, but her sticky, matter hair needed peeling off the pillow first. She smelled disgusting. She didn't know how she had got home or much of what happened the night before. One thing was for sure, she needed to change her dress. She staggered to the sink and washed her face. The water on her dry lips moistened them. It was then she remembered the cryptic phrase 'the hair of the dog' and suddenly knew exactly what it meant. Desperate for a drink to settle her stomach and stop the clanging in her head, she saw her usual drinking cup on her bedside table and remembered going to The Dragon to buy more gin. She remembered sitting in the corner, watching the goings-on in the pub, and that was where her recollection ended.

She dragged on a clean outfit as she pondered the conundrum of where she could find a bottle of gin on a Sunday. The law forbade the sale of alcohol on the Lord's day, but surely there had to be someone willing to part with a bottle for the right price.

Her head was a mess. She couldn't hold onto a single thought as she tried to create a mental list of people who could help her secure another precious drink. She was regretting her decision to not speak them for weeks if not months. Why would they go out of their way to help her now? She had become more of a stranger than a sister to Bronwyn, Francis and Mrs Jenkins.

The rusted garden gate creaked, and she looked out the window. It was Reverend Hughes—the last person she needed to see. *Will he ever stop mithering me?*

The door was open, but still, he knocked politely.

"Morning, Derryn," he chirped.

"Morning," she replied, wiping her face with her hand in an attempt to stifle a yawn.

"I was on my way to lunch with Mrs Jenkins, and I thought that I would pop in to say hello," he said.

"A bit out of your way isn't it?" quizzed Derryn, with a hint of contempt.

"Mmm, well, a little," blushed the minister. "I thought it would be lovely to see you. A lovely little place you have here."

"Don't patronise me, Reverend. You have never given me friendly visits. Why now like? As for the cottage, it's a hovel like all the rest."

The minister was aghast at her acerbic reply, but he recovered quickly.

"Mrs Jenkins has invited us—you and me—to have Sunday lunch with her."

"No, thank you. I am not feeling well today," muttered Derryn telling the truth, but realising that also seemed remarkably rude.

"You are right, Derryn. I should have given you some more notice. May I be frank for a moment?"

She nodded.

"I am visiting you with an ulterior motive. We are worried about you, that is your friends and me."

"No need to worry about me, Reverend."

She tried to laugh, but it came out a croak. She was thirsty, and her throat burned like fire from being sick.

"God loves you, Derryn. He understands your pain. He doesn't want you to suffer," he said kindly.

"Really, Reverend? Really? Then why did take my daughter from me, kill my husband in a mining accident, and then find a way to tell me that he allowed my spouse to stray from the marital bed with a fallen woman from the local brothel?"

"Really?"

"Really. Now, it seems everyone knew about Tiny's infidelity at the time, except you and me."

"You have to have faith that he loves you, Derryn."

"I've got to have faith? Is that all you can tell me? Is that the best that you can do? I don't want faith. I want peace. I want my child back. Can you do that for me? Can you?"

"No, Derryn, but God can. Maybe not in this lifetime but—"

Bitterness spewed forth from the battle-weary widow.

"Are you telling me that a God who tortures my soul like this is peaceful and loving? No, Reverend. You can share your fanciful ideas with a stupid fool who will fall for them."

"Can I pray for you, Derryn?"

"Certainly, Reverend Hughes. You can do whatever you want. But I'll tell you one thing, you will never, ever get me to pray ever again."

The minister stood up to leave. He walked toward her and put his hand on her arm and squeezed it. He didn't know what else to do. There was no kindness that he could bestow upon her that would ease her pain. It was one of those regretful situations where the onlookers had to watch the sufferer tumble to rock bottom. Reverend Hughes was fairly sure Derryn Evans didn't have much further to sink. All he could do was hope she survived the inevitable crash landing at the bottom of her self-inflicted abyss.

The minister had never experienced this irreverence or bitterness from one of his congregation. Nothing in his years of training at divinity school could prepare him for this day. He could find nothing to say that could comfort the woman. Her pain was tangible, and for the first time in his career, faced with such compelling evidence, for the first time, he found himself doubting what he was supposed to believe in too.

15

THE NIGHT AT THE DRAGON PUB

The money the colliery had paid to Derryn manged to last for just over six months, and that was only because she didn't eat much and drank instead. Fortunately, her spiralling drinking bill was mitigated by regularly frequenting The Dragon, where she had many admirers who would buy her drinks all night. She noticed the more effort she made with her appearance, the more drinks she got. There was a class about Derryn that men picked up on. She had dainty lady-like manners, was well-spoken and beautiful, when she made an effort. When she didn't make an effort, she looked more like a vagrant who had fallen on even worse times.

After her first disastrous stroll home from The Dragon, she disciplined herself to leave before she deteriorated into a paralytic state. She sternly told herself that she would leave the pub while she was still upright and go home to finish the job. That way she could drink until she passed out, hoping against hope that she would sleep until at least midday the following day.

She still didn't know who had helped her the night she collapsed in the lane. She doubted it was somebody who frequented her local because nobody had ever mentioned the incident. Her lump sum was dwindling. Instead of looking for work, Derryn began languishing in the pub in the afternoons as well as the evenings. Her womanly charm would be turned on full until somebody bought her a drink. She was reed-thin, and it was only her youth holding the ravages of the demon drink at bay. She had no food except for the little she scrounged at the local. At busy times, if she collected or washed the glasses when the staff were overrun, a sandwich was offered as payment. The usually proud young woman began to take less and less care of herself. She did the bare minimum with her appearance. She made just enough effort to secure the steady flow of drink.

She soon became desperate, driven by the reckless need to keep herself perpetually numbed by booze, and ideally, drunk.

"Right! Derryn!" greeted Walter the barman, cheerful as ever. "What is it for you tonight?"

Walter knew that she would not order anything but a glass of water, and then she would move over to her regular spot in the far corner to wait until somebody offered to buy her something. He had been watching her for some time now, and it was always the same routine. Some nights were quiet, and Walter could see the agony of her craving. She would become edgy, bordering on aggressive. Walter would say he needed a bit of help then pour her one on the house in lieu of payment in case she started bothering the other drinkers. On busy nights, there were plenty of rich pickings to be had, and she practically fell up the hill to get home before she collapsed.

Derryn was charming when she needed to be, but she was no longer the naïve girl who arrived at the village. It was evident that she was from a good home. It was visible in how she carried herself and the clothes that she wore. Nobody would ever guess the fortune that her family had amassed. She hadn't pleased her father when she announced her engagement to Tiny Evans, five years her senior. Thomas Morgan was deeply disappointed when he met the smarmy miner who had charmed his only child. He had not anticipated that his beautiful daughter, Derryn Morgan as she was then, would fall in love with a lout from a colliery village. Thomas Morgan was a doting father and had been in business long enough to develop a good nose for a man's integrity. When he met Tiny for the first time, instantly, he didn't like what he smelled.

Thomas had no qualms about his manual occupation. He respected anyone who did an honest day's work, but as any good father would he made a few enquiries about the fellow's provenance. He learnt that Tiny was actually Roger Evans, a well-known philanderer who had been married twice before. Thomas was a wise man who knew that to forbid his daughter would only harden her resolve to be with the man, so he gave her his blessing and went to straight to his lawyer to changed his will to read that if he died, Derryn would only inherit his fortune at the age of thirty. Her father reasoned that by the time that his only daughter reached thirty, Tiny would have moved on to his next mistress, deserting Derryn and his grandchildren. Everything that Thomas predicted would end up true. However, he and his wife died before they could witness it first-hand. Thomas would have been heartbroken if he knew that at this tender age, Derryn would be well on her way to destroying herself, without any influence from Tiny.

It was Friday night, and The Dragon was packed with hewers who had received their wages. Most of the men would drink away from a substantial chunk of their week's earnings, taking little home to their families. Misery and suffering abounded in the run-down miners' cottages. Tiny dwellings housed families of up to twelve. Neglected children struggled to get by with ill-fitting, patched clothing. The food and shelter were meagre—barely above subsistence levels. There were more affluent families to be found, as well, but very few. They were usually those who were followers of the Temperance Movement, who saved their money rather than drank it away.

A crowd of men had gathered around her table like vultures buying her one drink after the next. She had gained a bit of a reputation for being a good-time girl, at least when it came to talking—and drinking. That evening, Derryn was having a jolly good time and laughing at a joke. Her head was thrown back, and she looked carefree. She knew she could get more free drinks if she looked nice but forcing down food to keep her looks was proving to be a struggle. The lamplight was low in the dark pub, and it helped to disguise her impoverished physique. Bodies always jostled against each other near the counter. Men around Derryn loved using the crush to their advantage, rubbing against her body as much as they could. It was flattering, in a sense, making her a little bit aroused by the attention. She had never had this amount of interest levelled at her, not since her early days with Tiny. There was an attempt at music in a far corner. Everybody had to shout above the noise to be heard. Derryn was light-headed and happy, feeling like a queen holding court, surrounded by her flattering favourites.

A tall man walked in and sidled along the wall, aiming to squeeze his elbow onto the counter and catch the barman's eye. It had been a busy day, and he had developed quite a thirst. He watched Derryn from a distance but had more sense than to walk over and introduce himself. *She probably won't even notice me. She is clearly having far too much of a good time with her drinking pals.*

"Who is that? The blond little filly?" the newcomer asked Walter.

"Derryn Evans. A widow. She's a beaut, isn't she."

"Yes, she is," the man agreed.

"Mind you, compared to a lot of the tired old crones around here with most of their teeth rotted away, it's hard not to be a stunner?" Walter chuckled. "You new around here?".

"Yes and no. I bought Rodyr Hall over the other side of the woodland. Must have been a few months back now. But I've not ventured into town much myself, too busy, you see."

Walter laughed at the news of living in the hall.

"Then you have an interesting neighbour, Sir."

"Yes. Ludnow Gravis. I haven't met him yet. Don't intend to, truth be told. Heard plenty about him, mind. I'm sure he'd be more at home in an asylum with the other imbeciles, than in that farmhouse of his."

The man sounded a bit mean, but the barman brushed it off. Walter knew Ludnow was a strange chap, but, nevertheless, he never meant any harm. The barman decided it was late and the man was probably tired.

"I'm sorry. I forgot my manners. I'm Walter. Welcome to our valley."

The man nodded.

"Ellis Powell," came the reply.

It was after midnight, and quite a few people began to head for home. Most of the drunken crowd were from the rows, and they staggered back in a noisy group, bellies full of drink. The women stood screeching with laughter in the streets. They would holler loudly at the slower stragglers tottering behind them to keep up. First-floor curtains twitched all along the High Street as the irate shopkeepers grizzled about the commotion below, their one chance at a good night's sleep thwarted yet again. Most of the men continued to drink from bottles as they walked back, with their raucous women hanging on them for support.

As the crowd in the bar thinned out, Derryn sat at her regular table finishing her drink, somewhat disappointed that it looked like there would be no more gin for her that night. She cursed herself for running dry at home. Some point that evening, she had lost the money she had planned to use to replenish her stocks. Cadging drinks would be the only option that night it seemed. *It will be a long bleak Sunday if I can't find one of the other regulars to share some of their secret caches with me.*

Ellis Powell took a slow walk across the pub. Derryn noticed a tall man heading in her direction. As he drew nearer, she could see that he had neat brown hair and a thin moustache. She would have put him in his early thirties. He carried himself like a gentleman, and his whole person seemed to be tailored, from his perfect hair to his perfect boots. It was strange to see this sort of refined man in dive like The Dragon.

"Ellis Powell," he said he moved to shake her hand.

"Derryn Evans," she replied.

"You have a lot of friends, Miss Evans. I have been trying to talk to you all evening."

He smiled at her. She was fascinated by his immaculate row of straight white teeth. Better still, his clothing suggested he would have plenty of money for drink. *Maybe he'll treat me to a whole bottle before closing time if I flatter him enough.*

"Pleased to meet you, Mr Powell."

"I would like to buy you something to drink if you will allow it?"

"Thank you. That sounds wonderful," smiled Derryn. I didn't even have to turn on that much charm. Perfect.

It was the start of several rounds of drinks. They talked nonstop. Derryn thought it best to take a deep interest in the man, so he stayed longer. Eventually, Ellis announced that it was time for him to leave. There was nobody left in the pub and Walter was preparing to close.

"Can I walk you home, Derryn?" asked Walter.

"I'll be fine, thank you, Walter," drawled Derryn, swaying a little.

"I will walk her home, Walter," said Ellis. "I am heading that way. It's no bother."

"Are you sure, Sir?" asked Walter with concern, reluctant to see the vulnerable woman be escorted by a stranger to the valley.

"Of course, I am sure. I will ensure the lady gets home safe and sound. Please wait with her a moment while I go and collect my horse."

Walter and Derryn stood in frosty silence, he worried about her welfare, and her irritated by his fussing.

The rain from earlier in the evening had abated, and Ellis walked with Derryn to her cottage. He held his horse reins in one hand and her hand in the other so he could straighten her up when she faltered. Tempted by the free drinks from Ellis Powell, and the lack of liquor at home, she had not tapered her drinking as home time approached. Thankfully, she was still sober enough to know where she was supposed to be heading.

"I live here," said Derryn flailing her arm toward the cottage and then letting it flop against her body like a rag doll.

She was sure she could hear footsteps following them but was past caring to see if there really was somebody behind there.

Ellis knew precisely how vulnerable Derryn was. In the darkness, his lips parted to form a thin smile.

"What about a little nightcap?"

"I am sorry, Ellis, but I have nothing but tea."

"Not to worry. I am here to save the day—or perhaps night." His smile widened as he turned away from here. "I have a bottle in my saddlebag, I bought it when I was in the village."

Derryn's eyes lit up with excitement, "Well alright then. I could do with a touch more gin. I've been having trouble sleeping with it being so warm these past few nights. But let me tell you, I don't make a habit of letting men into my home at this time of night."

"I know. You're a lady with high standards," whispered Ellis. "But then again, nobody is watching."

The desire for drink pushed Derryn's recklessness up yet another notch. As Ellis led his horse around the back of the cottage, she flung open the front door, and after several clumsy failed strikes of numerous matches, managed to light the lamps.

Ellis strode into the kitchen area as Derryn giggled nervously as she passed him two teacups for the gin. She crossed the room unsteadily and started a fire in the stove. Ellis sat on the rocking chair, and Derryn sat on a kitchen chair in front of him, neither of them spoke. Derryn's confused mind was trying to think of something to say but then gave up. She used her mouth to slurp at the gin instead. Ellis refilled her cup several times, then he watched and waited like a patient vulture ready to tear her apart.

Derryn lost consciousness on the chair. Her legs flopped out straight in front of her. Her back was hunched against the backrest and her arms dangled at her sides. Her delicate chin dropped onto her chest, and her torso began to slide to one side.

"Derryn! Oh, Derryn!" called Ellis, the volume increasing with each syllable.

There was no response whatsoever. Ellis prodded her firmly in the belly. *Nothing. Good.* He grabbed her under the armpits and lifted her up. He was pleased her svelte little body was easy to manoeuvre into position. He put her knees against the edge of the bed, and let her thighs sink down as if she were sitting. Knowing where she would topple, he let go. Her back landed on the mattress with a thud. He realised he had made a mistake with the positioning. Her legs were awkward, where they were resting. He tried to pull her up the bed, but the space around the bed was a bit cramped, making it uncomfortable. *That will just have to do.*

Savouring the moment, Ellis slowly unbuttoned her blouse with his rough fingers. He pulled the fabric to one side, so her breasts were fully exposed. The sight aroused him as much as the thought of what was to come. He lifted her skirt until it was around her waist. Then he removed her underwear roughly, exposing a further expanse of creamy skin.

He hurriedly unbuttoned his trousers as he stood before her. *How lucky I am to find such a beautiful creature and have the pleasure of enjoying her intimately*. He took her violently, in a manner that she would never have permitted had she been sober. He couldn't care less as he saw her head roll with each thrust. Ellis Powell wasn't really bothered about pleasantries. With the deed done, he pulled up his trousers and left her as she was. Keen to cover his tracks, he picked up the bottle on the table, put away the two cups and fled the scene, grinning from ear to ear. Ellis couldn't believe what a lucky man he was. She was easy on the eye, desperate and loved a good drink. He knew exactly what he wanted to get out of this new relationship and how he was going to get it.

16

THE WORST SUNDAY

It was the worst Sunday of Derryn's life. In the early hours of the morning, she had awoken on her bed and almost naked. At that time, she was not yet in a fit state of mind to comprehend what had happened. Plagued with restlessness, she pulled the blankets around herself and after fidgeting for a while, went back to sleep.

She slept until well after midday, but eventually, it was inevitable she would become conscious of dizzy flashing lights behind her eyes and the frightful headache that began to invade her consciousness. She was forced to open her crusty eyelids and face the unwelcome day.

Her body was aching, and she had to get up slowly. It was then she noticed her blouse was unbuttoned and her breasts were exposed. Then she realised she was wearing nothing under her skirt. She looked at her underwear, lying on the floor next to the bed, and she began to panic. *What have I done?* She had an uncomfortable feeling of wetness between her legs and thought it was her monthlies. She checked, but it was not. Her fingers had discovered the wetness was clear. For the life of her, she couldn't recall much about the journey home. The last thing she could remember was preparing to leave the pub. There wasn't even a faint blur of memory after that.

Derryn didn't hear the gate open because she had put her head under the pillow to stifle any noise. Even the slightest sound felt like a hammer against her brain. The three hard bangs on the door sounded like thunder. She got such a fright that she sat bolt upright and perspiration bead on her skin. She decided to ignore the entry. It could only be the doctor or the minister, and she wanted to see neither of them. The pounding at the door continued.

It was no use. She would have to see who it was if the din were to be silenced. She quickly removed what remained of the previous night's going-out outfit and put on a nightshirt and dressing gown.

She went into the kitchen, peered through the small window to the left of the entrance. A handsome-looking stranger was standing outside, smiling. With reluctance she opened the door a fraction, thinking the sooner she could get rid of him, the sooner she could get back to bed.

"Er, yes?" she muttered through the small gap.

"Hello. May I come in?"

"No!" she answered, "Who are you?"

"You don't remember me?"

"No, I don't," she replied, "I have no clue who you are, Sir."

"Well, you invited me here last night. We had an enjoyable evening until I had to leave. You were quite generous with your hospitality."

Her mind was in a muddle. She delved deep into her booze-addled account but still had no memory of the events he referred to. She felt embarrassed, and the man was not helping her. In fact, he seemed to be enjoying her discomfort.

She looked down, not being able to meet his eyes or even think of the correct thing to say. She remembered her unbuttoned shirt and exposed breasts, the wetness and lack of underwear. Her mind was full of doubt. *Did I? Would I? What did this all mean? Who is this man?*

"Come on. Let me in, eh?" asked Ellis.

She shook her head at him and started to close the door. Through the narrowing gap, one of her eyes spied him opening his coat. She froze.

"I thought I would bring a little something to celebrate our new friendship," he said as he showed her the bottle.

He knew with the thick head from the night before, she would have killed for a drink to soothe her stomach and head. *This is like shooting fish in a barrel.*

"Come on, just a quick tipple won't hurt, will it?" he said temptingly as he used his bulk to push the door open and forced his way into the kitchen.

With great purpose, he went straight to the cupboard that held the gin cups and took them out. *How did he know they were kept there?* He poured a hefty measure of gin into one of the cups and gave it to her. *I know I shouldn't, but if it makes me feel better, it's got to be worth it.* He watched her with delight. She was like a small child. She took the cup in both hands and drained it in one gulp, not even bothering to offer her unexpected guest a seat.

"You seem quite partial to that. Would you like another?"

Without waiting for a response, Ellis filled her cup up to the brim. She drank the once burning spirit down like it was water. Thanks to her empty stomach, the drink rapidly hit the spot. Quite quickly, she began to feel better. The headache lessened. The nausea began to fade. Her courage grew.

She watched Ellis sip at his gin. He was staring at her, careful not to break his gaze as he tilted the cup to his lips.

"Who are you, and what are you doing here?" she demanded.

"I am Ellis Powell. The new owner of Rodyr Hall. You know the place. It's just over the other side of these here woods. I supposed that makes us distant neighbours. Can't you remember? I told you all about it last night."

The man was impeccably dressed and carried himself well. He seemed genuine enough, certainly not some sort of cad.

Derryn was paralysed with uncertainty.

"Come now, Derryn—"

He knows my name!

"—you don't have to be afraid of me."

He put the bottle down and sauntered towards her. Feeling threatened, she moved backwards until she felt her back nestled against the wall.

"There's no need to be fearful, my dear. What has got into you today?"

His patronising tone made the hackles rise up on the back of Derryn's neck.

"I have a proposition for you. I am looking for a maid, and you told me that you need to work now the money the colliery paid is almost exhausted. I will pay you a good wage to look after me."

The man made Derryn feel uncomfortable. *Why does he know so much about me?* The physical relief the fresh intake of booze gave her was quickly obliterated by her clearer thinking. It all made sense now. She was mortified by what had clearly happened between them after leaving The Dragon. Sadly, her lifestyle over the past few months had backed her into a corner. Derryn was out of options. The benevolent fund was all used up. She had no money for food or next month's rent. Worse than all of that she didn't know where her following few drinks would come from.

In a split second, she had weighed up her lack of options and nodded.

"Is that a yes?" he asked, a grin crossing his smooth, stubble-free face.

By now, he had her hemmed in, pushing his body against hers so that she couldn't escape.

She could smell his fresh breath and a clean body. He could have been attractive, but there was a darkness about him and Derryn found him menacing. She was right to. Quick as lightning, he rammed his hand down the neck of her nightshirt, searching for a firm white breast. He cupped one then squeezed her nipple as hard as he could until she yelped.

> "If I don't see you tomorrow, I will send Mr Swanson, my gamekeeper, to fetch you. Now, he is not a very pleasant man when he is imposed upon. He has unique powers of persuasion. I have seen him exercise it on poachers. Heaven knows what would happen if he turned his skills towards you! Do you understand me?"

She was visibly shaken. She began to tremble uncontrollably. Her wide eyes showed her fear. Intimidated, she looked off to one side and then nodded her head in defeat. Horrible feelings of terror had replaced those of her awful hangover.

Ellis Powell was a predator, and he could smell fresh meat. He felt a surge of adrenalin and lust course through his body, but he couldn't fulfil his desires now. Church had ended, and a few people would be walking down the lane. All she had to do was scream, and they would come to her aid. It was a risk he was not prepared not to take. There would be plenty of time for that later. He had her in the palm of his hand. There was no immediate rush.

Derryn was becoming ever more fearful of what lay ahead of her if she didn't submit to his demands.

As Ellis left, he generously left her the little bit of gin that was left. She drank it straight from the bottle, but it was not enough to calm her down.

Now, she noticed the stickiness and soreness between her legs. All she wanted to do was wash all the nastiness off her. She boiled up the water as quickly as she could and tipped it into the copper bath. Try as she might, she might be able to wash the filth off her flesh, but she couldn't erase the stain the truth had left on her soul. She lamented how she had tried and failed to stop drinking. *I have turned into a worthless, weak drunk. All the problems since Becca died are of my own making. It had been my conscious decision alienate everyone who tried to help me. I seem to have excelled at plotting my own demise. I frittered away a chance of a little freedom I had. Why didn't I pull myself together? I am not the first woman to lose a husband or child. They manage to cope. What a prize fool I am.*

Derryn's energy levels were low, and she washed her hair half-heartedly, but she was clean for the first time in days, and she felt better for it. The gin she had drunk earlier had worn off quickly, Derryn's guilt didn't prohibit her from obsessing about how she was going to survive the next day sober.

17

THE LANE TO THE HALL

Derryn set out for Rodyr Hall at six o'clock the following morning, just before sunrise, with only a linen bag with a few clothes. There would be nowhere to store the furniture at her lodgings at the farm—whatever they might consist of. Besides, the Watkins' lads would be unlikely to help her these days. Further, she didn't want the villagers knowing her business.

She dropped a note in Dr Pritchard's post box telling him she would have the next rent money for the following month by the end of the week and could he please keep the cottage for her. She was filled with a half-hearted hope that she would still be able to return to the cottage every few weeks. The one thing that had given her peace of mind was knowing her home had been paid upfront for six months. Now the money had run out, her situation was much more fraught.

Dark clouds filled the sky over to the west, mingling with the tendrils of grey-black colliery smoke reaching up to them. Over to the east, the sky was clear. Ellis Powell's farm was about an hour's walk from the cottage, and even though it was a road leading her to hell, the summery countryside hedgerow was still fascinating, fresh and fragrant. On any other day she would have been uplifted by the scenery, but today all she had to look forward to was an ominous meeting with Ellis Powell and perhaps the odious sounding Mr Swanson. The cheery sun began to rise in the sky, but Derryn was oblivious to its beauty.

She tried to push aside the memory of Powell's visit. Even though he had violated her while she was unconscious, no court in the country would convict him, and he knew it. All he had to say was that she had permitted it and that she was so drunk she couldn't remember giving her consent. Besides, even if she were foolhardy enough to plead her case in court, being scrutinised by a jury and named in the newspaper for all and sundry to gossip about would destroy what was left of her future. She would never be able to lead a normal life again.

She passed another farm as she made her way to the Rodyr estate. The yard was neat, and there was a sizeable barn nestled alongside on the left side and a pretty farmhouse towards the back. Two young lads were hard at work. To the right was a cottage garden with a row of fruit trees beginning to turn orange with the onset of the autumn. The farmhouse looked old. It was built out of rugged local stone, and even though it was in the early morning, the chimney was puffing smoke, and there were a few lights on inside. Derryn could imagine food being prepared on the cast iron stove, noisy family conversations around the table and the farmer returning from his early chores to have breakfast with his loved ones. There would be fresh milk with thick cream on it for their porridge, then eggs and bacon and fresh bread and butter. Two border collies who should have been on guard charged around the yard playfully. A rotund orange cat sat near gate post ignoring the dogs completely but watched Derryn go by with a resigned look in his eyes. The tabby's forlorn look reminded her of the reason why she was out so early, and a resigned look appeared on her face too.

It took Derryn another twenty minutes to reach the entrance to Rodyr Hall. In the distance, she could see the frontage of the imposing mock-Tudor house, such a popular architectural style with industrialists and their newfound wealth. She made her way up a gravel road lined with swaying weeping willow trees. *What a delightful place this must be in the summertime. Sitting under the cool shadows that the trees cast on hot days. I doubt I will experience that luxury, though.*

Derryn opened the gate and stepped onto the property of Ellis Powell. She walked up the driveway toward the house, she didn't dare knock on the front door, it wasn't her place as a servant, so she went around the side of the house and found the kitchen door. The courtyard was quiet except for the stables, where she saw some movement and lamplight. She knocked on the back door as loudly as she could. She couldn't tell if there was anybody inside. After a lengthy wait, the door was opened. A stern woman in a black dress stared at her in silence. *This girl is an unusually pretty one.*

"Good day. I am the new maid. Derryn Evans. I expect Mr Powell has told you about me?"

The woman remained quiet. Derryn felt the housekeeper's roving eyes, giving her the once over. Eventually, the stand-off ended. The woman swung the door wide open and finally asked Derryn to step inside.

The spacious kitchen was full of all the latest mod cons. The new arrival saw a cook working away at the stove, stirring busily. The smell of food was wonderful, but that was all that was welcoming. Nobody acknowledged her or attempted to introduce themselves. She stood alone, ignored for quite some time before the woman she presumed was the housekeeper spoke again

"Firstly, I will take you to your quarters," announced the housekeeper perfunctorily, "and then I will give you brief a tour of the hall."

They climbed the servants' staircase all the way to the attic on the fourth floor. The woman opened the door to a rather smart room with a slanted ceiling under the eaves of the house.

"My name is Derryn," she said to the austere woman in an attempt at warm conversation.

"I am Mrs Dutton. You will sleep here. Your working hours are from five o'clock in the morning until nine o'clock at night, unless the master requests you to work overtime."

She gave Derryn a hard stare to make sure she knew to comply with the rules to the letter.

"Of course," she said with a respectful nod for emphasis.

"You eat in the kitchen with the rest of the staff, but you will work as a housemaid. We will go through your schedule of duties. You are to make yourself as invisible as possible and avoid meeting anybody who is not a member of staff."

Derryn nodded again.

"Mrs Powell is very particular about the way her home is run."

Derryn's heart leapt into her throat. *Mrs Powell!* At that moment, she felt she had sunk to Connie Jones' level.

"Yes, she is a very agreeable person. There is a child as well—a three-year-old, but you will have very little to do with them if anything."

Derryn longed for something to drink to take the edge off her nerves. This revelation that Ellis Powell had a wife and child was quite a shock, and she had an overwhelming desire to flee. For now, she would have to stay put, terrified that Mr Swanson would find her as she made a run for it. *I shall have to bide my time. When I have the money, I will be able to catch the train to Cardiff. I'll surely find work in the city, but that bid for escape will have to wait until I am paid.*

Back in the kitchen, she was offered a cup of tea. It wasn't gin, but it would do. The cook poured some into a delicate teacup and handed it to her with a smile.

"Thank you," said Derryn, glad to see at least one friendly face.

Derryn's hands shook so badly when she took hold of it that it chattered against the saucer-like teeth on a frozen winter day. She promptly put the cup down to quell the noise. The cause of her tremors was two-fold. She was having severe withdrawals from the alcohol, and she was terrified to meet Ellis Powell again—Ellis Powell, the husband and father.

The kitchen door swung open, and a small man walked in, slamming the door behind him. His face was lined with wrinkles although the rest of his body suggested he was not particularly aged. He looked like somebody who had to live a hard life. When he opened his mouth to speak Derryn noted that he was missing teeth and those that remained were almost black. He was wearing a long mid-brown summer coat and a flat cap familiar to those that were popular with the Cardiff labourers.

"So, you got here?" he sneered.

She was surprised both by his knowledge of her visit and by his accent. He spoke like someone straight out of the Bristol Redcliffe slum.

"The boss said I had to fetch you if the weather was bad. Since it wasn't raining, I tended to some jobs around here."

When no one was looking at him, he winked at her suggestively. Derryn flinched, doing her best to hide it.

"Mr Swanson," called Mrs Dutton, "I have a favour to ask you. Please come to my office."

"I may still get to know you better yet," he whispered in her ear as he walked past.

"Go wait in the laundry room, lass. Stay away from Mr Swanson. He is not a very nice man at all," said the cook.

"I see. Thank you."

That was the second time in forty-eight hours Derryn had been told to keep clear of the man. Not that she needed much persuading to stay away upon meeting the fellow in the flesh.

Another person she didn't want to meet in the flesh was Mrs Powell. She would have to wait two weeks for that encounter.

Derryn had been dusting in the library when the door suddenly opened, and a new woman entered the room. She was gloriously glamourous, moving across the room like she was floating on air. She sat down at a large desk, opened a drawer and took out some writing paper.

Correctly deducing who the elegant mystery woman might be, Derryn tiptoed towards the special bookcase that doubled as a concealed door to the servant's corridor, but the woman called her back.

"Don't leave on my account?" she advised Derryn. "I will be gone as soon as I have written this correspondence. It's only a brief message. You can carry on."

"Thank you," replied Derryn.

"Are you new?" she continued.

"Yes, Ma'am."

"You may call me Mrs Powell," she said with a smile. "What is your name?" she enquired.

"Derryn Evans, Ma'am."

"Well I am pleased to meet you, Derryn," she said with a twinkle in her eye, "I am not nearly as fierce as they say I am in the kitchen, but I have to keep them on their guard else there would be chaos."

Megan Powell looked at the woman. There was something about her that was not typically common, perhaps it was the way she held herself or her accent. She noticed that she was an attractive mid-twenty-year-old, but she also looked world-weary.

"Are you married? Do you have children?"

"No. Mrs Powell—well not any more—" she stuttered. "My husband and daughter passed earlier in the year."

Mrs Powell face took on a look of deep compassion.

"I am sorry to hear that, Derryn. Forgive me for being such a busy-body," she said with sincerity. "You continue with your dusting. You won't disturb me. I don't want you to get into trouble with Mrs Dutton."

Derryn smiled and nodded, but felt sickened that she had been the means to an end for Mr Powell's infidelity.

The rhythmic scratching of Megan's nib on the paper stopped, and the drawer was slid closed.

"Goodbye, Derryn," announced Mrs Powell.

"Ma'am," she replied with a nod, not daring to turn round and look her in the eye.

Derryn had not thought or spoken about Tiny and Becca for a long time, and the memory of them crushed her chest like a sack of grain had landed heavily on it. She felt tearful and was enveloped with acute sadness. Depression settled over her again. It was a feeling that up until now she had chosen to quell with alcohol. That was no longer an option.

The next few days followed peacefully except for Derryn's craving for drink. Her hands still shook all the time, and on occasions, alone in her room at night, she was sure she could see strange apparitions that she couldn't judge as real or imagined. She perspired all the time, and by ten o'clock in the morning, her underclothes were damp with sweat.

Keeping the odour at bay was a challenge. She struggled to sleep, fighting with the twin problems of harsh reality and abstinence. For two weeks, she had been dry, but there was still the temptation to glug from a bottle in the middle of the night. Thankfully, her respect for the law and the need for a roof over her head was enough to tame her insatiable craving for liquor.

It would be a few days after meeting Megan until the inevitable rendezvous with Ellis Powell occurred. Her chore this time was polishing the bannister of the grand staircase. As he breezed past her, he snarled an instruction:

"Come to my study. Now."

Derryn froze with fear.

"Now, not next week. For goodness sake!"

Derryn followed him, dreading what might happen next

It was the first time that Derryn was allowed into his office. She had been strictly instructed by Mrs Dutton to never go anywhere near it, which suited her as she desperately wanted to avoid the beast of a man anyway. The first thing that she noted was a drinks trolley laden with bottles and bottles of alcohol. She couldn't take her eyes off them.

Ellis Powell watched and judged her every move, typical behaviour for any psychopath. He knew exactly how he would capitalise on her weakness, ultimately she would be a puppet—his puppet—and every time he pulled the string, she would do exactly what he wanted.

Derryn struggled to tear her eyes away from the trolley. He watched her inner struggle with amusement.

"This is a rather jolly room for relaxing, just as much as learning?" he suggested.

Derryn nodded, transfixed in the presence of alcohol.

"Perhaps you might want to visit here, at the end of the day, when your chores are done. Perhaps around eleven in the evening, when the hall is quiet?"

Derryn nodded again as Ellis paced across towards the drinks trolley.

"Of course, this is our secret. You won't talk to the other staff. Should my wife find out I may have to ask Mr Swanson to escort you back to the village."

Ellis Powell stared back at her, but she was not brave enough to meet his eyes. He took a glass off the trolley and poured himself a drink, then walked over to her and took a long, savoured sip, then wafted the glass under her nose so that she could smell the liquid. Her mouth began to water, and her heart beat faster.

Not needing to pull any more of Derryn's strings for the moment, Ellis dismissed her cruelly.

"I will see you tonight then. Eleven o'clock sharp."

She couldn't get out of the room fast enough. She was seized by a feeling of panic and was struggling to breathe. Then again, she would do anything to drink. He knew it—and she knew it.

18

THE SICKENING
STUDY

Just before their planned rendezvous, Derryn used
the service corridors to navigate herself to Ellis
Powell's study. She was terrified that somebody
would see her. Still, the passages were dark, and the
staff had retired for the night, so it felt worth the risk
for the prize at stake. She knocked softly on the door,
and he opened it. A crackling fire lit the room and
made it wonderfully warm.

"A little drink, perhaps?"

She nodded. He stood next to her. Judging by his
breath, he had clearly been drinking for quite some
time before her arrival.

"Why don't you take off that cardigan and get
more comfortable?" he suggested. "It's quite
warm in here.

Instinctively, she hugged the woollen garment closer to her body.

> "Come now, Derryn. You should not be shy of me. You weren't shy the first night we spent together."

Her mind was in turmoil. Awful as the idea was, she was fighting to recall that night. Try as she might, there was nothing, not even a hint. One thing was clear, she wanted something to drink.

She removed her cardigan and revealed her maid's uniform underneath.

He poured her a glass of amber liquid and passed it to her. She downed it, feeling the hot golden fluid run down her throat. The taste soothed her. She knew that she would soon feel the sensation of peace that she was craving. She drank one after the other. As she finished a glass, he poured the next until he thought she would be sufficiently pliable.

> "Now that I have pleased you, I think it is time that you pleased me, don't you?" suggested Ellis looking at her wryly.

He sat on a fireside chair and ordered her to stand in front of him. He pulled her down onto his lap.

> "I don't want to hear a noise from you, Derryn. Just to make sure, here's a little something to remind you."

Soon she'll pass out again, and that will become less of an issue.

"If you're not very generous tonight, Derryn, perhaps I will send for Mr Swanson to give you some training. Are you going to be generous?"

Too terrified to speak, she nodded. She didn't know who she feared most, Ellis Powell or the gamekeeper.

With relish, he began to touch her intimately. Sickened and scared, despite her woozy head, instinctively, she attempted to get away from him, but he overpowered her. Ellis Powell was insatiable, and for two hours he forced her to endure him acting out his every fantasy.

Derryn was mentally and physically broken by the time she left his study. She fled to her room and washed herself thoroughly, desperate to avoid falling pregnant. Downstairs, however, Ellis Powell was elated. He knew that he had the upper hand. He was well-practised in such matters, finding it far more expedient to abuse his maids to fulfil his physical needs.

His wife had made it perfectly clear on their honeymoon that there were certain acts that she would not participate in. Since the birth of his son, she had stopped sleeping in his bed, feeling utterly betrayed when she heard that her husband had spent nine months seducing a young girl throughout her pregnancy. Ellis found his wife's behaviour baffling. *How could she hold it against me? I am a man and men have needs.*

Megan Powell had every right to be infuriated. The young girl he had chosen to stray with during his son's gestation was her fifteen-year-old niece. Even Ellis had to agree it wasn't the best choice he could have made. Still, he couldn't resist breaking in a young nubile girl, and she had been such a willing student—eventually. As usual, a bit of charm, flattery and a lot of drink was all that was required. What more could a married man have asked for?

Every meeting with Ellis Powell was a further humiliation for Derryn. She had been working in the house for four months, and on most nights, except for when they had guests, he would request her company. Recently he had started taking more risks, even making her meet him in the room next to the one his wife slept in.

Sadly, Derryn's hopes to use her first wages to fund her escape to Cardiff had come to nought. Ellis had not paid Derryn for months. When he finally did give her some money, he threw a few paltry coins onto the ground and made her crawl across his study on her hands and knees to fetch it.

Derryn would spend days planning her escape from the house, but instead of paying her, he would put two bottles of gin next to an empty wage packet. She made pacts with herself. She made pacts with God. She prayed that she be strong enough to forego the liquor, but she wasn't. She was an alcoholic and wish as she might, she had no power over the substance, but it had absolute power over her. She was terrified of being without ample drink, and she ensured that she was as drunk as possible before Ellis arrived at her room.

By now, it was close to Christmas. Derryn was summoned to the kitchen.

"There is somebody to see you," said Mrs
Dutton. "You may use my office if you require
privacy for your meeting."

The housekeeper had worked for Ellis Powell for several years, and she was well aware of what he did to young women after hours. She hoped that the man who was visiting was there to fetch Derryn. She didn't know if the girl could suffer much more abuse.

Derryn opened the door to the small annexe and was met with a jovial-looking man who smiled brightly.

"I am Mr Austen, the solicitor in charge of
managing your late father's estate. How do
you do? I must say you took quite a lot of
tracing! I only found you when I asked
around the village. I was about to give up
hope until I went into the grocers. The

owner, Mrs Jenkins, thought you might be here."

"Good day," greeted Derryn.

"So, to the facts. You are Derryn Evans, née Morgan, the only daughter of Thomas Morgan late of Cardiff?"

"Yes, Sir," she confirmed quietly as she looked down, fidgeting with her hands.

She had been estranged from her family in their final years, and she had felt guilty about casting them aside.

"I am sure you are aware of the conditions stipulated in your father's will and what is due to you at the age of thirty. It is my job to keep in contact with you and ensure that I can find you when it is time to transfer the funds."

She nodded.

"You are aware that you can draw upon these funds in case of an emergency. The terms state I am required to assess the situation, and upon my advice, the bank will agree to the transfer of funds."

Derryn nodded, although it was the first time that she heard that she could draw money in case of an emergency.

"I don't understand why I now have access to this fortune."

"There is a clause in the will that says that should cause your husband to die, and you become a widow, you can draw on this fund within reason. Your father obviously didn't want you to suffer as a widow."

Derryn nodded slowly. Her father, as always, had thought of everything. Remembering him, she smiled weakly.

"I am going to leave my details with you. My offices are in Cardiff, but if you are unable to get to me there, please send a telegram, and I will come to you."

"Thank you, Mr Austen, I appreciate your visit. This is quite a lot to take in. Forgive me."

"Derryn, your father always worried about you and wanted the best for your future," he advised kindly. "I think he had some concerns about the suitability of Mr Evans as a husband."

Her father had been right. She had settled for a selfish, feckless adulterer. Tensed to breaking point, her throat burned with guilt and woe rather than gin and whisky. Tears welled up in her eyes. She knew it would be pointless to even try to utter a word. Not a sound would come out.

"Well, I'd better be off," said Mr Austen uncomfortably. "You have my card."

He left without her saying goodbye. From what he had seen, it seemed he had just arrived in time. Why she had not jumped at his offer confused him. He put her reluctance to act promptly down to the shock of his unexpected visit. He made a note to check on her regularly. She seemed in great need of assistance.

Mr Austen was mistaken. Derryn was keen to act, but by sending a telegram. And within a couple of days, she took decisive action about her future.

19

THE ESCAPE THROUGH THE WOODLAND

The December air that Sunday afternoon was bitter, and a thick layer of snow and ice blanketed the land. The weather had not improved for days, but Mr Austin's news had galvanised Derryn's mood. She had decided it was time for her to flee the horror of Rodyr Hall.

Early in the morning, she tiptoed to the kitchen and quietly slipped outside, crossing the courtyard slowly to avoid slipping. Although it was risky, she stuck to the winding road that led towards the woods, thinking her progress across the icy ridges of the neighbouring ploughed fields would have been desperately slow. Plus, there was nowhere to run for cover if she were spotted.

Against the grey sky, she could see the silhouettes of leafless trees with their blackened branches, and sturdy trunks standing in deep snow. Occasionally, she would hear the crisp crack of a branch break and fall, the weight of the snow too much for it to bear. The fresh air hit her lungs and cleared her head. The numbing daze she had been living in for months left her. Now, she had a proper plan, an escape route, and she was determined to grab that opportunity. *It is time to free myself from all the terror that tortured my days and nights being under the roof of Ellis Powell.*

As she reached the woodland, she was aware of the high-pitched bleat of an animal in pain. She realised that the noise was coming from behind a rocky outcrop. She darted behind a thick tree trunk, her heart knocking at her ribs. She had a horrible feeling it might be Mr Swanson out hunting for meat for the kitchen. Desperate to know what she might face, she peered around the tree trunk and saw two men walking toward the spot where the noise was coming from, both armed with rifles. Shocked, but needing to find out more, Derryn made sure she was well hidden behind the tree, then carefully looked on. The two men looked like they were patrolling the perimeter of their respective land since there was a wire fence between the two of them.

She was right about one thing. The man on the right was the gamekeeper, Mr Swanson, his distinctive hat and coat clearly visible. Plus, he was the man patrolling Ellis Powell's land. The other man, however, was not Powell. Judging by his height, and the style of his clothing, it was Ludnow Gravis. She decided the land he was patrolling probably belonged to the pretty little farmhouse she had seen some weeks earlier. Feeling a little braver knowing Ludnow was nearby, she moved her head a little further out from behind the tree. From her improved vantage point, she could see a small deer stuck in the fence wire. The panicked thing was whining for dear life. In the distance at the edge of the woodland, Derryn spotted the mother pacing and snorting, irate and helpless. Thinking back to her horror and powerlessness when she saw Becca, Derryn was filled with deep compassion for the animal. For Derryn at least, the two parents formed some sort of silent bond, forged in the hot fire of heartbreaking pain.

Ludnow moved forward slowly, not wanting to frighten the little creature. It was so young that it still had white speckles on its back. He was only a couple of feet away from. Swanson, who stood on the Rodyr land, stopped dead in his tracks. She watched Ludnow check if his rifle was loaded, then balance it against a fence pole. He put his hand in his pocket to remove something from it. Derryn watched Swanson lift the rifle to his shoulder and gaze down the long barrel and aiming for the animal. She was certain that the first man who got the opportunity was going to put the foal out of its misery. From where she stood, she heard the distinctive click of Swanson's gun as it was locked and loaded. The helpless mother was becoming more distraught, letting out a low guttural grunt. The harrowing sound of the mother dreading the death of her foal was too much for Derryn to bear.

"Swanson! No!" she yelled.

The surprise voice made Ludnow raise his head. The interruption cause Swanson to lose his aim as he pulled the trigger, the shot wildly missed the deer.

The slug hit the ground and shards of ice sprayed into the air between Ludnow and the deer. The crack of gunfire was deafening compared with the stillness of the day. The noise echoed throughout the valley.

Gravis didn't flinch at the shot. He sank onto his haunches and using the tool in his hand, snipped the wire, then gently untangled the tiny creature. The little deer took a moment or two to realise it could move freely again. It suddenly bleated joyfully and bounced lightly across the snowy field to its mother. Now reunited, the mother led her offspring to safety with haste, blending into the far side of the distant woodland. Derryn noticed how Ludnow had performed the rescue with the utmost gentleness and sensitivity. One more, she had seen that beautiful smile develop under the brim of his hat as he worked to free the little thing.

Swanson took no interest in the deer. It was Derryn who was now in his sights. The murderous look in the gamekeeper's eyes had not gone, but rather hunting a new target.

Derryn thought it best to curtail the escape for now. Swanson was bound to look for her, and if he found her out at large things would not end well. At best she would be captured and returned to Ellis Powell who would be keen to mete out further punishment. She tiptoed away from her viewpoint, fearful of each delicate footstep on the crunchy frost. Despite her meticulousness, one footstep met with a thin fallen branch. The wood snapped loudly, giving her position away to the two experienced hunters. Both men turned and stared in her direction. Their eyes fell upon her figure against the skyline. They both stared at her. Swanson gave her a menacing glare born of hatred, but the gaze from the loner Ludnow Gravis was one of unrequited love.

Derryn was terrified. She ran back to Rodyr Hall to seek safety from Swanson, alas in the home of the other monster in her life, Ellis Powell, and not Mr Austin in Cardiff.

Predicting her next move, Swanson took a shortcut through the woods, planning to strike when she returned along the path to the hall.

20

THE RETURN TO RODYR

Swanson cornered her as she ran into the courtyard. He was a small, wiry man but exceptionally strong. He dragged her over to the stables where nobody could hear him.

"Were you spying on me, you wench?" he rasped.

"No! I was out for a walk, and I heard the animal."

"You wouldn't be lying now, would you?"

She shook her head, tears welling in her eyes. He shook her hard as he threatened her.

"You weren't trying to run away from the Master, like, were yer now?"

She was almost hysterical with fear and began shaking.

"I will gladly tell him where I found you, and you better have a good story like."

He shoved her, and she went sprawling across the stables landing in the dirty straw.

Radiating hell itself, he stared at her with contempt. As he left the stable, he spat at her face and called her a whore.

Derryn did her best to clean herself up. Feeling utterly defeated, she went back to the kitchen.

Ellis Powell visited her room in the early hours of the morning. She had hoped that he would stay away, but once again, Derryn was out of luck. Powell opened the door forcefully, grabbing it just before the handle smashed noisily into the wall. Instead of his usual quiet controlling sadism, he was filled with a feral fury. He was still in his riding clothes, and he was wielding a riding crop.

"So, you were out like a harlot fantasising about Ludnow Gravis?"

"No, I wasn't," she cried.

"Swanson told me that he found you watching the damned fellow."

"No," she cried again.

"I don't share my trollops with my neighbours," he snarled as he closed the door behind him.

He brought the riding crop down upon her. She felt it slice down on her flesh. He brought the crop down upon her another three times on her back and shoulders. The angry deep welts oozed a little blood through her nightclothes. He wanted to thrash her until she begged for mercy, but she didn't. Instead, she collapsed in a heap in the corner, in silence, shielding her head in her hands. Ellis Powell stormed from the room. It seemed the sight of blood alone would be enough to satisfy his ugly dark desires that night. Derryn dragged herself to her bed.

When she woke up, her face was still swollen from crying. She was in so much pain she could hardly move. She summoned all her will to get out of bed. Her nightclothes were stuck to her wounds, and she had to soak them off. The water stung like fire, and she cried all over again. Still, she managed to get herself looking shipshape. She went painstakingly slowly, not wanting the wounds to reopen. Finally, she manoeuvred herself into her uniform. She wore a couple of thin vests underneath her blouse, hoping it would hide any blood. She got to breakfast ten minutes later than usual.

Swanson stared at her over his teacup and winked. It was very early in the morning, but the master had must have told him about the beating. Derryn was sick with humiliation, and the next thirty minutes would take all the courage she had left to sit at the breakfast table and pretend that she was fine. Keen to hide the truth, she put on a front and smiled and chatted to the other staff members. Although she was in frightful pain, she would not give Swanson the satisfaction of seeing her flinch.

Within a week of the terrible beating, Derryn discovered that she was pregnant. Ellis Powell had been nowhere near her for two weeks, but it was not out of a sense of clemency. He and Mrs Powell had taken a journey to London to spend some time on the social circuit. Although Ellis was away, Derryn was not out of harm's way with Swanson on the property. She did her best to avoid him, or at least not be alone in his presence.

Derryn was terrified to tell Ellis Powell that she was pregnant, unsure of his reaction. Her condition did at least offer a glimmer of hope that she might be sent away in disgrace. However, Ellis was an unpredictable fellow. He might just punch her hard in the stomach and resolve the matter that way. There was one positive development for Derryn. The constant agony of her wounds reminded her she needed to be free of her alcohol craving. It was the only way to diminish the power Ellis had over her.

The latest bottle of gin he had supplied stood next to her bed unopened.

On Ellis' return, it took Derryn two days to pluck up the courage to broach the subject with her brutal boss. She knocked on his study door in the middle of the afternoon and went in without being invited.

"You know not to come here in the day," he warned in a controlled even voice.

She closed the door behind her.

"I am pregnant," she confessed.

He leaned back in his chair contemptuously and looked her up and down.

"And you think that the child is mine?"

She couldn't believe the words had come from his mouth.

"Of course."

"Well, what about old Swanson?"

She shook her head and began to cry.

"I will get you a drink. Stop making a scene. What if my wife comes in?"

He poured gin into a class and gave it to her, but she pulled her head away from it.

"No, thank you," she whispered.

He grabbed her by the arm, dug his fingers so deep they almost met with bone and thrust the liquor under her nose.

"You will drink it, or I will make you."

She screamed in pain. He released his grip and clamped his hand over her mouth instead.

"I suggest you don't try to get my wife's attention."

Derryn was snivelling in terror. Ellis gave up using drink as a weapon and chose another from his arsenal.

"Shut up, or I will kill you right here, right now," threatened Powell. "I have done it before. I can do it again. No one who matters ever misses a servant. People always believe my tale that the poor unfortunate girl left in a hurry to care for an ailing mother."

He grabbed Derryn by the throat, his fingers now crushing her windpipe. As she started to choke, he said:

"If you tell anybody about this bairn, it will be the end of you. Do you understand?"

"Yes," she croaked.

Derryn had hoped against hope that Ellis would banish her, but it was now clear that would not be the case. She dreaded to think what evil scheme the cruel man would dream up next for her.

He let her go with a shove, and she had to sit on a nearby chair before she fainted.

"Now, what shall we do about you? I don't like the idea of losing you. But you are of no use pregnant, are you?"

Her eyes widened.

"Now, I don't want you to panic, but I will arrange some tablets from Dr Pritchard. He usually takes care of these little inconveniences for me."

"Dr Pritchard?" she whispered, stunned that he would get tangled up with a violent man like Powell.

"Yes, we are old friends. We went to Cambridge together. He has helped me out of a few of these predicaments before."

"But an abortion can kill me?"

"Well, either way, you certainly will not be having my child. Dr Pritchard will terminate the pregnancy. It is a straightforward procedure. And don't seem so shocked, you are not the first girl that I have had to do this for. Actually, it's fortuitous you brought this to my attention at this early stage. It can all be dealt with while you go about your regular duties."

Derryn could hardly breathe as Ellis told her more of the plan.

"In the morning, I will send Swanson to Dr Pritchard with a note. The good doctor will prescribe some pills for you. If you do not do it Dr Pritchard's way, I will allow Swanson to do it his way. Do you hear me? He has done it before, and he will do it again even if he has to beat the child out of you himself. Now, Get out!"

Derryn struggled to get to her feet.

"Get out and tell Swanson to come here now. And don't ever come to my study unless I call you! Do you understand me?"

She nodded without looking back at him.

"And go and splash some cold water on your face. I don't want the staff seeing you like you are. It makes me look bad."

She closed the door behind her, dreading another encounter with Swanson.

Fifteen minutes later, Swanson swaggered into the room. The common gangster was proving his worth.

"You are looking for me, Guv?" he asked in his common vernacular.

"Yes, go over to Dr Pritchard in the morning. You know, for the usual thing."

"Yes, Guv. I'm wondering Guv, is it worf it, like? Maybe I can take care of it like I did the last one. I can save ya a few quid."

"I have just broken her in, Swanson. It's not time for her to go yet."

"I was just finking, Guv."

"I don't pay you to think Swanson, but I will pass her on when I am finished with her."

Swanson chuckled and rubbed his hands together:

"Thanks, Guv. Thanks very much!"

That night, Derryn lay wide awake praying that Ellis Powell would not come to her room. She feared the abortion. She was scared to stay in the hall and was too scared to run away. If she stayed, she would live a life of one horror after the next. Swanson and Ellis Powell had hinted at the grisly end that had met other women from the household. If she tried to escape, she knew in her gut somehow, she would be discovered and beaten. Or worse.

She wished she had discussed the withdrawal of funds with Mr Austen when he visited. She deeply regretted not travelling back to Cardiff with him. News of the emergency funds had dismayed her. *Life would have been quite different if Becca and I had left the mining village. If only I had been bolder!*

Derryn had missed dinner in the kitchen that night. She had no courage to face Swanson. The weeping welts on her back had stuck to her clothing once more and needed dealing with. Fear had quashed her appetite yet again. Despite her dire situation, she had no interest in the gin beside her, knowing that keeping her wits about her was no vital. She picked it up and opened it, then opened up the window and quietly started pouring it on the sill. She watched the poison trickle away, glad to see the back of it. It was the lowest moment in her life, but also her strongest. She would never touch alcohol again. It had brought her to this bleak predicament. It had robbed her of all her dignity. It was close to taking her life, but at the eleventh hour, she had triumphed. She resolved to pour some water back in the bottle to make it appear as if she were still partaking in the demon drink.

A gentle knock at the door startled her. She backed herself up against the wall, staring at the door as it was firmly opened, her heart thumping in her chest.

Mrs Dutton put her head around the door.

"Derryn, may I come in?"

"Yes, please do. I am sorry I didn't come to supper, Mrs Dutton."

"I have brought you some tea and something to eat. You must be famished. It's been very long since breakfast," said the kindly housekeeper.

"Thank you, Mrs Dutton."

"I overheard Swanson and Mr Powell talking late this afternoon of their plans for you. Terrible things have happened in this household at the hands of those two. You must leave tonight."

Derryn nodded.

"Swanson is to go to Dr Pritchard's first thing. He will be back just after breakfast. You should get away now, under cover of darkness. Dress up as warmly as you can and get back to the village and safety. It's bitter out there. Is there somebody who will take you in?"

"I used to have friends there. I pray they will show pity on me. I was awful. The grief made me push them all away after Becca—."

"I will leave the back door unlocked. Slip out quietly. Be quick now."

"Thank you, Mrs Dutton."

"It's a pleasure, lass. It's time to put a stop to Mr Powell's cruel way with you."

21

THE ADVICE OF MRS DUTTON

Depression and hopelessness threatened overwhelmed her, but she kept on hearing the hopeful words of Mrs Dutton.

"You have to get away tonight."

She wore as many clothes as she could, partly to keep warm, and partly to avoid being slowed down by a bulky bag, then let herself out through the unlocked door. She pulled the big brim of her bonnet down around the sides of her head. Thick snow drifted down peacefully, and there was no moon. The countryside was pitch black. She silently sped along to the entrance gates, occasionally glancing back. The house was in darkness. She prayed that Ellis Powell was sleeping soundly in his bed. As she closed the gates behind her, she prayed she would never set eyes on Rodyr Hall ever again.

Derryn knew that she would have to throw herself on the mercy of one of her old friends, but she still had to decide which one, Bronwyn or Mrs Jenkins. Bronwyn had a house full of children and didn't need another mouth to feed. If she went back to the miner's rows, there would be a lot of gossip and embarrassing questions. Thankfully the bairn wasn't showing yet, else the tongues might never stop wagging. Her best ally would have to be Mrs Jenkins. She had no family except for her husband, and they had put her up before in her hour of need.

Derryn could only hope that the woman would forgive her for the heartless display of self-interest that had surely ruined their friendship.

The difficulties would not end there. She would not be able to shield herself from the cruel humiliation to come. Even if she could explain her pregnancy away to violation, nobody would be understanding or forgiving. It was the oldest gentleman's sport in Great Britain, forcibly despoiling the hired help.

She hoped for once that things would work in her favour. All she needed was a safe haven for a day or two until she could get a telegram to Mr Austen, the Cardiff solicitor.

She was clueless about the matter of the child. Having the baby adopted couldn't guarantee its future. Deserting it to grow up in a beastly orphanage was equally cruel. She couldn't stomach the idea that she would inflict such great suffering on an innocent child. It would torture her for the rest of her living years. The other option was equally unpalatable—risking death from complications from an illegal backstreet abortion.

The ice on the road was treacherous, and twice her feet had slipped from beneath her. Her arms flailed uncontrollably. Luckily at the last moment, she found her balance. Despite the fight to stand upright, the core temperature of her thin little body was plummeting. Clouds of white vapour from her laboured breathing escaped through her mouth and nostrils. She couldn't feel her feet or her face. Her numbed nose began to run like a tap, and she had to wipe it all the time. The hot, heavy perspiration that had formed inside her clothes when she first fled the hall at breakneck speed was now beginning to freeze, chilling her to the marrow.

As thick white flakes of snow drifted around her, the forlorn-looking fugitive began to lose track of her bearings and how far she had travelled along the lane towards the village. Thankfully, a black building started to loom out of the darkness. Derryn realised that she had reached the farmhouse. Although there were no lights on, the dark structure on the horizon was just enough of a clue to let her determine her position.

She crunched through the snow trying to remain on the road, although it was difficult to see where the path ended, and the shallow drainage ditch in the verge began. Occasionally, she stepped into the dip and lost her footing, but luckily, she didn't twist her ankle. She strained her eyes to see where she was going. While she might have just been able to navigate the road, she was still panicking about how she was going to navigate the next forty-eight hours of her life.

The dark farmhouse was close, and she could just make out the farm gate. She thought about sneaking into the barn and settling there for the night, then thought better of it. The animals would wake up and alert the owner to her presence, which might risk getting shot. Besides, she was out of courage.

Her only hope of surviving the night was to knock on the farmhouse door and ask for help, and hope it was proffered. Cold, tired and weak, she was preparing to give up on the idea of escaping to see Mr Austin. She slowly manoeuvred herself toward the farm gate. She planned to lean on it for a while, gather her strength then push onto to the farm door.

She was only a few yards from the gate when she felt her boot heel hook onto something under the snow. A concealed tree root had tripped her up. She saw the ground raced towards her face. She stretched out her arms to break the fall, but to no avail. Worse, her head crashed against a rock hidden under the blanket of whiteness. A dreadful pain shot through her skull. Lights popped in her brain. With that,

Derryn lost consciousness. Her head lay at an odd angle against the stone, and hot blood trickled down her ice-cold face staining the snow beneath it and freezing one drop at a time.

Lying beside the farmer's bed, two border collies began to snarl softly. The man was conscious of the low growls. It meant they could hear something out of the ordinary out of human earshot. At this time of night, that was seldom a good thing. The restless dogs stood up, then started pacing the room. They moved to the window and stuck their heads under the curtain, trying to see what they had picked up on. Unsuccessful, they turned to the door and start yelping to go out. The farmer shushed them, and they lay down at the door for a few moments, noses to the ground and sniffing the air that came in from under the door. Within a few minutes, they resumed their restless behaviour. Peering out of the window, the farmer saw nothing. *What time is this to want to go out!*

"Alright. Alright. Calm down. What have you heard, boys?" he asked them.

He stood up and put on a big warm coat and pulled on his boots. He bent his well-built body so that he didn't hit his head against the frame as he passed through the doorway. The dogs scampered ahead of him. Despite his bulk, quiet as a mouse, he opened the front door, and his face was hit by a wall of freezing air. *Damn.* He turned back into the kitchen and threw some big logs onto the fire. In their haste, the dogs charged past him eager to get into the yard. They collided with his legs with some force.

He watched them hop around on the cold ground, then head straight to the farm gate and start barking frantically. After lighting an oil lamp, the farmer strode over to them.

"Come on, fellas," he said, "what is upsetting you?"

He opened the gate to allow the dogs to run free, but they didn't go far. They moved less than two yards, then began barking even louder than ever. As he watched them pawing and nudging something dark the snow. *It looks like a heap of fabric. Perhaps some tarpaulin that fell off a cart?* The gloomy little lamp wasn't up to the job required of it. The strange light played tricks on the eyes. He didn't see the woman until he had almost fallen over her. Bending forward, holding up the lamp to take a better look, he was shocked. At his feet was a person—a woman judging by the bonnet. He noticed another dark patch in the snow—a different one—a bloodstain. Putting a hand on her cheek, she was so cold he was sure she was dead.

The farmer gathered up the woman and carried her into the farmhouse. He lay her icy body in front of the fire. She didn't move. He had to control himself in order not to spiral into a panic. The massive logs on the fire had started to burn ferociously, and the kitchen was warm. He got down on his hands and knees and turned his attention to reviving her. He peeled the soggy bonnet from her face and recognised her instantly. *Derryn*. Her face was snow white and serene, but her lips were turning blue at the edges. Alone, in his farmhouse, Ludnow Gravis heart was filled with fear. *This can't happen.*

Silently, he manoeuvred her out of her coat. He rested his ear on her chest. He prayed for a heart but could hear nothing. Her chest was ice cold. There was no sign of breathing. He held her tenderly by the wrist. He was sure that he could feel a feeble pulse through the thick rugged skin of his workman's fingertips. However, it could have been his imagination, and he was too afraid to hope.

Her hair was a frozen mass of water and blood, and although the fire was getting bigger, the woman was not getting any warmer. He rushed to the water pump and filled a massive cauldron and put it onto the fire. Then, he went to the shed and grabbed an old copper bath from days gone by.

He checked on her and saw her breathing was improving, although she was still unconscious.

For him, the kitchen was sweltering. He removed his greatcoat, revealing a nightshirt over some long johns. Impatiently he waited for the water in the cauldron to heat up. Knowing the wet clothes were hampering his endeavours to save her, gently, he removed her clothing. He saw the severe welts on her back and shoulders, still oozing and raw. *Hot water on those is going to feel like liquid fire, but what option do I have? This was my only opportunity to save her. The injuries will have to be dealt with later.* He lay her back down on his greatcoat, then filled the bath with warm water. He gently picked her up and transferred her to the copper bath. Almost her body entire body was submerged in the water. He cradled her with one arm, and with the other, he held a jug. *Try not to let the water trickle over her face,* he washed out the blood from her frozen hair, hoping to get a better sense of the severity of the wound. He was pleased to note it was one of those tiny cuts that bled a lot more than it might be expected to. It would soon heal. He put his hand over her heart, and against the palm of his hand felt a beat that was slower and stronger. He was filled with relief and fought hard to choke back his tears.

"Thank God above!" he rejoiced. "Oh, thank God!"

Putting his mouth to her ear, he tried to rouse her back to consciousness.

"Wake up, Derryn," he whispered, "come on, wake up."

Far in the distance, there was a voice. There is was then again. At first, Derryn thought it was her mother, but it wasn't. Her head was spinning. More than anything else, she wanted to fall asleep. Still, the voice kept nagging at her until she could ignore it no more. She felt herself speeding faster and faster through a dark tunnel towards the voice. It began to change, becoming a deep rich sound, its reassuring tone coaxing her towards it.

"Derryn. Derryn, listen to me. You are safe.
Nobody is going to hurt you. Come on,
Derryn. Wake up for me."

With his latest attempt to revive her, Ludnow was relieved to see she had entered the realm of consciousness once more. Derryn could feel her mind thumping inside her skull. She opened her eyes slowly. The light from the kitchen lamps stung her eyes, making her blink and then clamp her eyelids shut. She felt the water lapping against her skin. Choosing to open her eyes slowly to become accustomed to the light, she found herself lying naked in a hot bath of water next to a massive fireplace. Terrified, she crossed her arms over her chest. Against one cheek, she felt the fire was burning hot. Along the stone walls hung copper pots hanging against the wall. The firelight sparkled against the metal, giving the whole room an ambience of warmth and comfort. A man was kneeling next to the bath. He was supporting her; his face was very close to hers. Derryn was trying desperately to place who the face belonged to. She stared at him through the narrow slits of her eyes. With his piercing blue eyes, he was the most handsome man that she had ever seen. *It's Ludnow Gravis— the Sin-Eater!* Still stunned and confused, she muttered:

"Where am I?"

"You are in my home, and you are safe," his deep and gentle voice reassured.

She lifted her hand out of the water and touched his face, gently stroking his cheek with her delicate fingers. The act was so tender, Ludnow was taken by surprise. He desperately wanted to kiss her, but he knew that it was not the right time.

"Thank you," she whispered.

"Can I make you some tea? A strong cup, with lots of sugar," he volunteered with a smile.

"Yes, please," Derryn replied, then lay limply and still half-dazed.

Ludnow gave her the tea, and she accepted it with shaky hands.

"Your body must hurt," he said, gazing towards her back.

Lacking the energy to talk after her ordeal, she nodded.

"Have you eaten anything today?"

Derryn shook her head. He went to the table in the centre of the room and cut a piece of bread and spread thick farm butter on it. He fed her two bites, but then she shook her head.

"No more, please— I feel ill."

Ludnow had looked after enough animals to know her flesh wounds needed tending to if infection were to be staved off. He left her in the water while he went to find a cloth to clean them with. The head wound had stopped bleeding. He dabbed at it gently with some clean water and carbolic soap to wash out the grit in the gash. The terrible cuts on her back and shoulders were severe. He helped her out of the bath and sat her with her back by the fire, hoping the warm, dry air might make them form a protective scab more quickly. *Dr Pritchard might need to prescribe something for her if the oozing doesn't abate.*

"I'll be back as soon as possible," he told her before bounding upstairs.

In the room where she was to sleep, he made a fire, waiting until the golden kindling flames started to take hold of the logs. He returned with one of his nightshirts and helped her put it on.

Then he wrapped her in a thick down quilt, sat her in front of the fire, and dried her hair.

By the time the process was finished, Derryn was exhausted. She lacked the strength to hold her head up. He helped her up the narrow wooden steps and opened the door to a small room. She climbed onto the bed.

He made her lie on her stomach and pulled down the large the nightshirt until he could see the deep gashes on her back. The oozing had stopped. He covered her up again.

"You are safe here, Derryn."

"Thank you."

Ludnow didn't answer. He gave a simple nod of the head and smiled down at her.

22

THE CHANGE OF PLAN

"Should we change our plans, Guv?" asked Swanson

"Yes, I think we should," replied Ellis Powell.

Swanson's chest filled with pride. He was always delighted when 'the Guv' appreciated his opinion. Ellis revealed his take on the problem of Derryn Evan's escape to his henchman.

"She couldn't have got far in this weather. She is either dead which would be ideal, or she made it to the village and is hiding out with somebody. Someone in the village has to know. Persuade the information out of them if you need to," instructed Ellis.

"Fink we should ask the doc, Guv? She might have needed help for them wounds from the riding crop?"

"It is unlikely that she will call upon the doctor for help. She is aware of my relationship with him and will anticipate him alerting me to her whereabouts. Besides, we don't need the doctor to know more than he needs to. Only call on him as a last resort?"

"Should I make contact wiv the weird fellow, that farmer next door?"

"You can ask him, but I strongly doubt she would go there. The villagers fear him and don't go near his property. I am sure she will make her way towards the shops or Miner's Row."

"Yes, Guv. What should I do if I find her?"

"Take her to your gamekeeper's cottage, just like we did the other girls. No special treatment for her."

Swanson grinned from ear to ear. The words were like music to his ears.

The sky had cleared after the snow. However, the sun provided no warmth. A light wind blew across the fields. The snow and ice on the roads were still treacherous. The gamekeeper wore his thick coat and hat, and some tatty grey fingerless gloves, gripping his fingers deep into his palms to keep them shielded.

Swanson was delighted to have some excitement in his dreary life. Being a gamekeeper on a remote country estate was not his idea of excitement. At least today was going to be a change from the dull routine he had followed of late. Swanson didn't enjoy the countryside, but circumstances had forced him into isolation. He longed for the old days in Redcliffe and the adrenalin-charged life of crime. Swanson and Powell's friendship went back many years when he met 'the Guv' at a brothel in the heart of one of Cardiff's dockland slums. Both of them had rather unusual tastes in women and the services they were expected to provide. Swanson was an expert in selecting the most vulnerable and needy souls to indulge the sick desires of Powell, targeting the laudanum, opium and alcohol addicts who functioned in a hazy desperate fog. These desperate women tended to be more willing to suffer a wide range of abuses if it meant they could perpetuate their habit.

Instead of Ellis Powell's marriage, reducing his abusive desires, it exacerbated them. They were forbidden fruit. Megan Powell made it clear that if he crossed the line with her, she would rip her fortune from under his feet. Nothing spoke louder to Ellis than money, and he made sure that he treated her with the utmost respect from then on. The birth of his son did little to move him to emotion, and the conception of the child was a miracle. On one of his rare droughts of sexual activity with the fallen women, in desperation, he approached his wife and was delighted when she granted him a reception.

Megan was aware of her husband's adulterous proclivities, but only with their maids. Putting on a brave face in public and to her family, she preferred to withdraw from the marital bed than try to fight for a divorce. She wasn't happy when her husband hired the thug that was Swanson. Something about the man unsettled her, and beneath his forced polite demeanour, she sensed pure evil. Since her husband had hired the man, Ellis had developed an odd passion for hunting and he and Swanson would regularly spend weekends at the hunting lodge in a remote area of the estate. There was never much evidence of their game kills being brought back for the cook to deal with. If they weren't at the lodge, it would be an overnight trip to Cardiff.

Becoming increasingly irritated by their erratic and disrespectful behaviour, Megan vowed to keep tabs on the pair. She decided that the next time Ellis and Swanson went to Cardiff together, she would take a ride out the hunting lodge to see what was so exciting about it.

'It's what men do.' Ellis had whined when she confronted him about his new penchant for hunting. She remained unconvinced. Since when did a city slum rogue and a Cambridge-educated dandy appreciate the joys of nature together—for days at a time?

"I see another maid has left us," said Megan Powell to her husband over dinner.

"Really my dear? I honestly haven't noticed," He replied, looking straight into her eyes. "You should really have a word with Mrs Dutton, my dear, she is clearly mistreating them."

"Yes, it has come to my attention that Evans, the young widow, has left. I rather liked her."

"How many times have I told you not to get sentimental about the staff?" said Ellis, concentrating on his meal.

"I come from a home where we were proud to care for our employees. It is the way my father raised us."

Ellis nodded.

"Of course, I agree with you, dear, and that attitude is commendable," he patronised.

Megan bristled. Under her ladylike demeanour, she was furious. The staff turnover was concerning and given she and the co-workers treated each other with respect, it wasn't difficult to pinpoint the reason why they left the Powell household in droves.

"I will take the next maid into my personal care, and I will move her closer to my bedroom."

She watched Elli's face with interest.

"Well, if you want to do that, I can't stop you. Of course, I completely disapprove of moving servants out of their quarters. Rather, I was considering allowing Swanson to oversee the staff, rather than Mrs Dutton. I think he would make an exceptional butler."

Megan looked up from her plate straight into his handsome, calculating face.

"You will not bring that man into my home as long as I pay the bills. In fact, I think that he has outgrown his usefulness. He is not performing the tasks he is hired for. Poachers seem to ride roughshod over our land. You never seem to bring any game back to be served at the table. I am putting him on a month's notice."

Megan could see him fighting to maintain his composure. His face reddened, and even at a distance, she could see him clenching his teeth. Trying to undermine her will, he deliberately disobeyed the intention of her instruction.

"I will talk to him and tell him that you are unhappy with his performance and that you will reassess his conduct at the end of next month."

Megan didn't acknowledge the suggestion. They finished their dinner in silence, and she left the table without excusing herself.

The following morning at the farm, Ludnow Gravis saw a shadowy rider in the distance. He had just finished feeding the animals in the barn, and he gave orders to his two farmworkers, the twins, John and Robbie Baker, to clean the troughs and fork the hay. Out of compassion, a few months ago, he had given the two boys and their ailing old mother a small tumble-down cottage on the periphery of his farm. The Bakers had fallen on hard times, and their desperation had forced them to talk to the curious loner. It had been a good move for the family. Ludnow didn't charge them rent since it had been little more than a stone shelter for animals when they moved in. The boys had worked hard to smarten the place and make it habitable. Both lads were reliable and hard-working, and their help made the farm more manageable.

The horseman stopped at the farm gate. Ludnow recognised it was Swanson, the repugnant gamekeeper from the Rodyr Hall. They had met on several occasions but never exchanged more than a few words. The last time had been when Ludnow had rescued the young deer from Swanson's bullet. *I am confident that man is no gamekeeper. He would have raised the ire of any farmer.*

Without wasting time, Ludnow walked towards him politely, giving a nod of acknowledgement.

"Ellis Powell has sent me," announced Swanson without a greeting.

"We was worried about one of the maids working for us," the gamekeeper continued. "Perhaps you have seen her?"

Ludnow looked at him, offering no response. Swanson probed desperately for more information.

"She left the hall late a couple of nights ago, like, telling Mrs Dutton she was visiting an old friend, she did. Someone in the village, I believe. She hasn't returned, and we fink that some fink awful has happened to her."

The dogs had bounded to the gate. They were agitated and aggressive, and they placed themselves between Ludnow and Swanson, protecting their master.

"Well, have you seen her?" asked Swanson annoyance in his voice.

"No. Now, keep moving, Swanson. I have nothing else to say to a man like you," warned Ludnow.

Swanson was enraged by the reply. He turned the horse around and sharply dug his heels in the animal.

It whinnied and shot forward. Ludnow felt guilty for that feeling his terse reply had compelled the disgusting human to take his anger out on the innocent animal.

"Boys," Ludnow called out.

They ran towards him.

"We've had a visitor in the house for a short while, a widow from the village, Derryn Evans. I found her in the lane a couple of nights ago, badly beaten, and almost frozen to death. Heaven knows how she got there. You won't have seen her, she's in the spare room, recuperating. Keep this to yourselves, though. Some men from up at the hall are after her. I suspect she was trying to flee their clutches. If I am not here to keep an eye out and something untoward happens, my shotgun is behind the kitchen door. I don't trust those devils."

The boys looked on open-mouthed.

Drawing a blank at the farm, Swanson continued his enquiries about Derryn's whereabouts at the doctor's, pointedly ignoring Ellis' instructions.

"Doc, she walked out into the snow. She was coming to see somebody in the village. But the night was cruel, Doc, and surely she would have got here half dead? Did she come to you for help?"

"No, Swanson. I haven't seen her since she left the cottage when she'd drunk away the last of her benevolent fund, leaving me without a tenant. I was glad that she was taken in by Ellis. I thought that he may— grow fond of her."

Dr Pritchard smirked. Swanson smiled conspiratorially and winked at him. The doctor didn't really like Swanson, he saw him as a common brute, but he served his purpose. He was imperative to the success of their 'hunting weekends'. Working in the country would be so dull if there were no distractions.

The three men had the perfect symbiotic relationship, Swanson sourced the women and guaranteed their silence. Ellis supplied the venue and entertainment for them all, and the doctor ensured that no children were born of the delightful experience. There was the problem of the ladies who refused to participate, but Swanson took care of them. Ellis rewarded his gamekeeper by passing the women onto him when he had finished with them.

Swanson subtly canvassed far and wide within the village, but he was given with the same answer time and again. 'The widow had left months ago. Word had it that she had gone to work at Rodyr Hall. There had been no news since she left the cottage and if he found her, would he please let them know.'

By four o'clock, the weather was dark and miserable--so was the gamekeeper.

He had given the situation a lot of thought, the only shelter along the lane between Rodyr Hall and the village was the farm. Is Ludnow Gravis telling me lies?

His last stop on the way home was The Dragon. He stepped inside the warm and inviting pub. Surveying the area, he saw there were only a few patrons. The rest would arrive after work. An icy blast struck the few drinkers close to the entrance, and they gave Swanson the evil eye until the door was firmly closed. Walter was tending the bar, and he was not particularly happy to see Swanson. He didn't like the coarseness of the fellow.

"Pint of draft," he ordered, no hint of a smile on his face.

Walter put the drink in front of him.

"I am looking for Derryn Evans," he whispered.

"Not been in here for months, pal," Walter replied.

"She took off in the night a couple of days ago. We are worried she's frozen and lying dead somewhere."

"I told you. She doesn't come here anymore."

Everybody in the village was wary of Swanson. In fact, they were warier of him than the devilish sin-eater, Ludnow Gravis.

"When last did you see her?" asked Swanson.

With growing exasperation, Walter ignored him.

Swanson tried to quell his rage, but he had to have the last word, and it was a fatal mistake,

"Ellis Powell wants her back. He has taken a liking to her."

Swanson didn't get the desired response from Walter, so he pushed a little more, with a gravelly whisper.

"She's pregnant wiv his child, and he doesn't want her dead."

Walters didn't react. He started to serve a customer further down the bar.

Swanson knew that he would get nothing out of the barman, so he finished the draft and banged the glass loudly on the counter and slammed the door on his way out.

Walter had grown fond of Derryn and had been troubled by her slow deterioration after her little girl's death. Although he knew alcoholics would do anything to get another drink, he still felt guilty he did not do more to help her.

He knew that Ellis Powell was a pig. His reputation preceded him. It had become known to him via some of the more liberal ladies that after they spent a night with him, they were lucky to have escaped alive.

Most of them had left the village quickly after the encounter and Connie Jones had told him she feared for her life. One night, when she was a bit worse for wear, her loose tongue had revealed her ordeal.

> "Walter, let me tell you something about Ellis Powell. Not a word of this is a lie, I have to tell someone. It's burning a hole in me. He took me to a cottage. Weird place it was. Looked disused. Well, except for one purpose. That Swanson was there too. They both beat me senseless, only got excited when I was bloodied up and begging for mercy. You gotta warn the girls Walter, yer gotta warn them like, that Ellis Powell is still going to commit murder like, don't go near him."

It seemed so farfetched at the time. Ellis Powell was a well-to-do man with a roving eye for the ladies. There was nothing strange in that. What was strange was that he chose to liaise with such a coarse fellow. It wasn't a typical master and servant relationship.

Walter had watched Ellis hovering around Derryn the first night that he met her in the pub and his menacing insistence that he would get her home— alone. When the barman heard that she was working at Rodyr Hall, he was deeply depressed. He had tried to get a letter to her a few times, but she had never replied.

Edwyn, Bronwyn's husband, arrived at the pub around about seven o'clock.

"Scotch, Walter, please."

"Of course. Oh, and just before you take your seat, can I have a word out the back?"

Edwyn raised his eyebrows. Walter didn't mess about, he was serious.

"Derryn Evans has disappeared. We were right. She did end up at the hall. Swanson has just been in here asking after her. Supposedly Ellis Powell is searching after her, and she is pregnant with his child, Edwyn."

The hewer looked astonished. It seems Derryn managed to sink even lower! Edwyn sank his whisky in one glug.

"You know what news of an illegitimate child means for a married man like Powell, tied to his wife's financial apron strings."

Edwyn didn't stay for a second drink. He walked straight back to the rows, he needed to speak to Bronwyn.

"God above have mercy!" cried Bronwyn. "Can that woman sink any lower?"

"Shush Bronwyn, we cannot have the kids hearing this. They remember her as she was."

"Edwyn, she has no money. Where could she go for 48 hours in this weather? She is probably lying somewhere frozen to death. Edwyn, don't sit there like a sack of spuds. Answer me!"

She paused to give him a moment to speak, then lost patience again.

"Should we put together a search party, Edwyn?"

"Give me time to think Bronwyn, for goodness sake. I will speak to a few people I trust, I will take Will, George Watkins and his boys will help us for certain, perhaps Mr Jenkins, if he's up to it. He cares about the girl, but he's getting on a bit."

Bronwyn was hysterical.

"Go and see the sin-eater, Gravis, Edwyn. His farm is close to Rodyr Hall. Maybe he has seen something. While you're there see if you can search his farm. I don't trust that man as far as I could throw him!"

Edwyn put his arms around her and held her close, rubbing her back as he spoke.

"I'll ask George Watkins to speak to him. He knows him well."

"What if you don't find her tonight? What about work?" asked Bronwyn ever practical.

"Don't you worry about that lass, that's my problem," he smiled and kissed her on the forehead. "We will find her, one way or the other we will find her."

Swanson stood before Ellis Powell and gave him the bad news that his extensive search had been fruitless.

"Mmm," sighed Ellis, "I would be lying if I told you that I wasn't disappointed. This is really not the best work you have done for me."

"Guv, I spoke to everybody, I promise I did. But nobody could tell me any fink, like. They haven't heard from her in mumfs, "

"You had better come up with a good idea, my man. The wife has given me notice on you."

Swanson frowned. He thought he was irreplaceable, but he was mistaken. *Well, I didn't expect that. What happened to me being the Guv's right-hand man. How has Megan Powell become involved? How could the Guv let her make the rules?* Powell preferred his puppet to see him as all-powerful, not a hen-pecked husband living in his wife's shadow.

"Relax, Guv. I will fink of sum fink overnight. You know--sleep on it like."

"Don't sleep too long, Swanson. Find her."

23

THE CONVALESCENCE

Late in the evening, Derryn awoke in the warm bed where she had been convalescing. The down mattress and pillows made her snug, and she was loathed to get up.

The room was small, and the walls were whitewashed. There was a small window that had pretty lace curtains hanging in front of it. The floor was made of wide wooden beams. There was a large bright rug on the floor and hanging on the wall was a cheery tapestry of some flowers. In the corner was a wooden rocking chair which reminded her of the one in her old cottage.

Next to the bed was a small bureau with an oil lamp on it. Derryn was surprised how pretty it was and that the room had such a feminine touch for a man of the land like Gravis.

She tried to get up, but her legs trembled underneath her. She grabbed onto the desk to force herself upright and walked one small step at a time to reach the door.

She took an age to descend the narrow staircase. When she reached the bottom, she shuffled into the kitchen, it was dark outside. She had no idea of the time, but the fire was burning, and the kitchen was warm.

Ludnow turned around and smiled at her.

"You are awake at last."

"Can I sit down?" she asked shyly.

"Of course," he took her by the arm and helped her into the chair. Not even in the years of her marriage to Tiny had she ever felt this secure. By instinct, she knew that this man would be protective of her, even if she was a stranger to him.

"I am making tea, and I am going to give you one with milk and two sugars as well. You are shaking, you need the energy."

He turned to pour the water then looked over his shoulder to quip:

"No arguing about feeling ill this time".

"That will be lovely," she answered. "What time is it? What day is it?"

"You've been here since the early hours of the morning, and you've been for nigh on two days. You were very weak when I found you. It's about seven o'clock," Ludnow answered as he stirred the drinks.

"How did I get here?" she said, looking around the kitchen. She saw the copper bath still standing in the corner, not quite sure why it was familiar.

"That's my question," he replied with a smile, "If you were coming from the hall, it's a miracle you got here on that treacherous road - given the terrible state you were in when I found you."

Despite warming to the sin-eater, Derryn felt vulnerable at the mention of the hall. She didn't want to talk about what happened to her--and definitely not reveal that Ellis Powell had fathered the child in her.

Ludnow passed her the tea, and she drank it slowly in silence. He was a very private man, and he treated others with the same respect. He wouldn't pry into her business.

"Actually, the hounds heard you outside the gate. We went out, and they lead me to you, lying in the snow. You must have got that bump on the head from banging your head on a rock when you collapsed."

Derryn was shocked as she heard more about her flight from the hall.

"You're lucky these two found you just in the nick of time," said Ludnow as he ruffled the thick fur on the back of their necks. "It was the middle of the night, and I was fast asleep.

"Oh, my word! I have put you out, Mr Gravis," she said, feeling her blushing cheeks burn with embarrassment.

She watched him ladling soup into a bowl for her. It seemed so incongruent—the man who was reviled by the villagers had opened up his home to her.

"Not at all. Except for having to defrost you, you've stayed out of my way since you arrived."

He gave a rich laugh that made her smile.

Derryn finished the soup and watched him tidy up the kitchen. He was comfortable with himself, and she too felt comfortable in the silence. Homely as it all was, she recalled that she was desperate to take the train to Cardiff and meet Mr Austin. If she were honest, she wanted to leave Wales altogether.

"I need to get to the village, Ludnow. I have people there who will take care of me until I leave."

Secretly crestfallen she was going so soon, he hid his true feelings with a mask of cheery helpfulness.

"Yes, I can take you in. Who will you go to?"

"I was thinking of Mrs Jenkins, the grocers' wife. She has always been very kind. My best friend Bronwyn from the rows will have me, but I will be a burden. She has too many mouths to feed. George and Franny Watkins might also take me in, but they too have a full house."

"Yes, of course, I will take you. Just tell me when you are ready to go."

"Thank you. I am sorry I have been such trouble. By the morning I will be gone. I promise."

Derryn was relieved that he didn't ask her further questions. She hobbled off towards her room.

"Allow me to help you up those stairs," volunteered Ludnow.

"Yes, please," she smiled.

"We must look at those cuts on your back in the morning before you leave. They need to be kept clean."

She nodded but couldn't meet his eyes. The embarrassment was too great.

Ludnow helped her up the stairs. Nothing was intimidating about him. He made no suggestive remarks when he helped her into the soft bed. He made no attempt to take advantage of her vulnerability. With a kind expression, he stood back and gazed down at her.

"How do you feel now?" he smiled.

"Much better, thank you."

"I will fetch some more tea and sit here until you are asleep."

"Yes, I'd like that."

When Ludnow came and back sat down, he had brought a lamp and book with him as well. She snuggled into the soft bedding and fell asleep in a matter of minutes. Ludnow looked up from the book from time to time, and when he was sure that she was settled, he left the room and closed the door softly behind him.

Having a visitor felt strange to Ludnow. He had been alone for many years. Except for the farmhands,

George Watkins and the postman, he hardly saw anyone regularly. Everyone else in the village poured scorn on him whenever he was seen. *Whatever pain I feel being shunned now, it's nothing compared to what I have had to face in the past. She never did, though.*

He thought back to Derryn and the first time that he had seen her. She seemed so different from the people in the village. Refined. She wasn't rough around the edges like the other women in the row, and he wondered how she had ended up with a collier. Plus, it was evident on that day in the old family kitchen that she had deep compassion for people.

She seemed more girlish then, softer, with curves and proud eyes that shined despite the grief. Ludnow knew that she lost her husband and her child within months of each other. Her life must have been a living hell.

Noticing he was becoming morose, something he was often prone to, he put on his coat and walked to the barn to check on the animals. He kept himself busy and his thoughts at bay by filling the drinking troughs. It had been a long day, and finally, tiredness was catching up with him.

On his return, he went directly to his bedroom and washed. He climbed into bed, leaving his door open in case Derryn needed him during the night. Even the dogs slept in front of her bedroom door for the time being.

In the morning, Ludnow knocked on the door with the tip of his shoe.

"Come in."

"I don't do this for everybody," declared a grinning Ludnow, holding a fully laden tray with both hands.

A surprised Derryn propped herself up with her pillows in anticipation, and he put the tray on her lap. He had made her a breakfast of bacon, egg, crumpets and tea. Derryn was surprised at how hungry she was and wolfed down the breakfast at a pace that impressed Ludnow.

"You are getting better," he said with a grin.

She nodded and returned the smile.

"What is time is it?"

"Early," said Ludnow before he glanced at his pocket watch. "Seven o'clock."

"Good. I need to leave here and get on my way. I have already stayed too long and can impose upon you no longer."

With a tinge of sadness, he explained how he would set her off on her way.

"Right, I need to go and collect some lambs from Bert Woodhead next door. It's about a fifteen-minute ride in the wagon. He's meeting me at the northern fence. I don't want to send the youngsters. I want to see them for myself before he sets a price. The Baker lads will look after you, and when I get back, I will take you to Mrs Jenkins. That gives you a bit of time to get packed. I can tend to those wounds on your back as well."

"Really, there is no need. The ride is enough, thank you."

"I have got hot water on the fire for you and Robbie will fill the bath when it boils. It will take another ten minutes. I insist that you clean up those cuts. Don't take any chances with them. I don't want you adding blood poisoning to your health woes."

She was overwhelmed by his thoughtfulness.

"Alright. I will tend to them. Happy?"

"Good," he said with a smile, then picked up the tray and the plate that barely needed a rinse. He was pleased to note Derryn had wolfed down every morsel.

"You are an excellent cook,"

"Am I? Well, that's good to know," he chortled.

She watched him leave with the tray in hand. *What an incredibly kind man he is.*

From her bedroom window, she could see a tremendous black block of cloud moving surely toward the farm. The weather was rolling in, and there was all likelihood that it would start to snow by noon. She got up slowly and found her carpetbag next to the bureau. She took out fresh clothes and went downstairs to the kitchen. Ludnow was as good as his word. He had left her fresh towels and several bars of carbolic soap. Robbie saw her through the window, kicked off his muddy boots then came in to fill the tub with steaming hot water.

There was a roaring fire in the hearth. The boys had done a wonderful job to ensure that she wouldn't get cold. She wondered how she would ever repay the kindness, and it played on her mind for quite a while.

She pulled the curtain closed and undressed with mechanical movements, ensuring that she didn't crack open the healing wounds.

For the first time in months, she got a proper look at herself. She looked at her body. Her breasts had shrunk markedly, and she could count her ribs. Her angular hips and shoulder blades stuck out. Despite the pregnancy, her stomach was indented.

She saw her face in the mirror, sunken cheeks, hollow eyes and hair had lost its shine and bounce. She was ashamed of the person who stared back out at her. When she stopped visiting the Dragon to cadge free drinks, she had really let her appearance go. She wondered what Ludnow thought of her decline.

Just after the break of dawn, Swanson had decided to investigate his last likely lead. Knowing there would be a long list of jobs to do around the farm, he stood on the rise and watched Ludnow Gravis leave the house. After what seemed like an age, finally, Swanson was elated. It was about time that his luck turned. He had been waiting for hours for the opportunity to get into Ludnow's house and take a snoop around. He was convinced that if he were to find Derryn anywhere still alive, it had to be there.

The chances are slim that she would hide in the barn. One of those two idiot farmhands would have found her by now. Besides she would be starving and would have to come out for something to eat by now. No, I need a different approach.

Instinctively, he knew what plan he would follow. It was time to dust off his stealthy housebreaking skills. First, he planned to search through the house, and if he got no results, he would strong-arm some information out of the youngsters. Threatening to break a few of their dead old Ma's fingers will quickly focus their minds.

Derryn dozed off as the healing water enveloped her. In truth, she could have stayed at the farmhouse for much longer, but how could she ask that of a total stranger?

She felt depressed at the thought of leaving but pushed the thought to the back of her mind. Wincing, she dabbed some carbolic soap suds on the welts on her shoulders. Distracted by the stinging wounds, she wasn't aware of the gate opening or the dogs scratching at the door. Ludnow had left them inside the house, but they were so friendly she had already made up her mind that they would be utterly ineffective as guard dogs. She heard the crunch of gritty footsteps outside and watched the door handle moving down slowly. By now, the dogs were barking. *It must be one of the Baker boys, surely?* Derryn was about to shout that she was undressed to the person outside but didn't get the opportunity.

The door swung open, and the gnarly figure of Swanson stood in the doorway. When he saw her, he was too excited to close the door, not only to have found her but to have found her naked and vulnerable. The sight of her flesh filled him with lust. He wanted to take advantage of the opportunity presented before him, whether Ellis Powell liked it or not.

The dogs jumped up against Swanson barking into his face, but he batted them aside with tremendous force leaving them a little stunned for a moment. He grabbed Derryn by the hair and dragged her up and out of the bath. She wanted to scream for help but couldn't. Swanson drove his fist into her stomach. The agonizing blow winded her into silence. She had doubled up in pain. Swanson's boot kicked her forward, so she landed face down on the stone floor. Instinctively, the dogs sensed a kill and put themselves between Derryn and Swanson. Shep went for his arm and bit down hard. Swanson howled and knocked the dog off him. The smell of blood reached the nostrils of Dixie, and the powerful collie launched itself into the air going straight for Swanson's throat.

By the time the twins reached the kitchen, the air was permeated with the smell of dogs, blood and death. Swanson lay on the floor, having choked on his own blood.

On hearing the commotion, Robbie forced the possessed-looking and bloodied dogs out of the kitchen and closed the door behind them. They were scrabbling at the entrance, still barking as if their lives depended on it. Their killer instincts had taken over, and they were eager to rip out what was left of Swanson's throat. Robbie stared at the door, leaning against it to keep it closed as he fought to slide across all the metal bolts.

John rushed to Derryn's side and fell onto his knees. He rolled her over onto her back. Having landed on her face once more, it was coated in blood once more.

She was still gasping for air, clutching at her belly, delirious and groaning. She looked an awful sight.

Unconscious, Derryn was a dead weight, and young John struggled to lift her.

"Help me, Robbie. Don't just stand there.
Can't you see I'm struggling? We need to get
her upstairs! Now!" he shouted.

Robbie turned away from the door to help John, but what he saw made him gasp. He had no experience with women, and he was petrified. As well as a gashed head, Derryn had a cascade of blood running down between her legs too. Stunned, he didn't know what to do.

"Come on. Let's get her to a bed. She can't
stay here, with—him!" commanded John,
staring at Swanson's lifeless body.

She hung between them like a rag doll. Her feet dragged against the floor, smearing the trail of red behind her. Being nearest, they lifted her onto Ludnow's bed as gently as they could. John, with the calmer head of the two, grabbed a nightshirt and thrust it up between Derryn's legs, then covered her with the eiderdown. He began dabbing her head to clean the blood off her face. Robbie looked on, motionless. Losing patience, John bellowed at his brother.

"Robbie—go and fetch, Ludnow—now! Take the horse. Hurry."

Since hearing of her disappearance, Edwyn and George had planned to make a thorough search of the road to the hall and numerous outbuildings in the vicinity in various states of disrepair. The lack of light had hindered their search, and reluctantly they decided to hold off the search proper until the following morning. The two men had sent sons Mikey and Willy on ahead that night. They had been instructed to walk to Rodyr Hall, and at sunrise, begin their detailed search from the hall end of the lane towards the village. George and Edwyn would begin their search from the High Street. The two parties would meet each other somewhere in the middle, hopefully with good news.

George and Edwyn agreed that it was unlikely that Derryn would stray off the road. Thick hedges lined each side of the lane. They correctly assumed traversing them when cold, weak and afraid would have been arduous. They felt they would be more likely to find her somewhere in the lane. If they didn't find her along the road, they would arrange a search party and comb the fields and meadows and look for her. No one mentioned the word 'her body', but secretly, they all thought it.

Robbie reached Ludnow as he lifted the last lamb onto the wagon.

"Ludnow, you have to come home right now. It's the widow staying with you, Ludnow. Something terrible has happened. A strange man turned up and attacked her. John says to hurry."

Ludnow had heard similar words before, and his heart began to pound in his chest.

"Give me the horse. You come back on the cart," instructed Ludnow.

Before Robbie could even answer, Gravis grabbed the reins from the boy and pulled him from the horse. The lad was paralysed with fear. He watched the galloping horse cut across the field with Ludnow riding like a lunatic, risking the horse and himself.

As Ludnow reached the farmhouse, Edwyn and George reached the farm gate. They watched the horse gallop into the yard, Ludnow opened the door and flew into the house with the dogs barking hysterically at his heels.

"John!" he yelled.

"Here!" came the reply from upstairs.

Ludnow jumped over the bloody corpse of Swanson and took three stairs at a time to the landing. He saw his bedroom door open and heard John moving around.

"In here, Mr Gravis," John shouted again.

John was pleased had to good sense to cover Derryn and clean her face up a little.

"She's bleeding badly. She needs a doctor."

Ludnow whipped back the covers to see for himself, then flinched. Judging by where the blood was coming from, it was clear that Swanson must have been acting on Ellis Powell's orders.

"Go!" shouted Ludnow, "Bring him here. And hurry. I'll stay with her."

John stormed down the staircase and went tearing into the kitchen. George and Edwyn stood at the open door hesitant to go inside without an invitation.

"Where is Ludnow?" asked George when he saw the boy.

"Can't talk. We need a doctor for the widow."

John climbed onto the horse and raced as fast as he could toward the village.

George and Edwyn peered into the kitchen. It looked as if there had been a war. Furniture was turned upside down. There was water all over the floor, with the ogre Swanson, his throat eviscerated, lying dead in the centre of it all. They didn't know what to make of the scene, or who was responsible for such an atrocity.

"Ludnow. It's George Watkins. Can I come in?"

"Up here in the bedroom," boomed Gravis' deep voice.

George and Edwyn sidestepped the corpse of the gamekeeper, trying not to look at it, then headed for the stairs. A startled Ludnow Gravis turned to look at them.

"My goodness. What has happened here, lad? Tell me. I am here to help you," said George gently.

"He tried to kill her George!" said Ludnow, through gritted teeth, his loud voice now quiet and wavering with the strain of explaining what had happened.

"Who tried to kill her?"

"Swanson, the gamekeeper from Rodyr Hall. Don't ask me why."

"I think I might know," said Edwyn. "Walter at the Dragon told me—"

"—Derryn!" whispered Ludnow as he firmly pushed her shoulder down towards the mattress in an attempt to revive her. Her head lolled loosely. She was now completely unconscious.

An anxious Gravis turned to the two men, looking for advice but received none.

"What's wrong with her?" asked George.

"I don't know."

Ludnow lifted the sheet.

"Oh, dear God! And those long slashes by her shoulders?" asked George on seeing the frail and battered body.

"All Ellis Powell's handiwork. He whipped her for disobeying him, the savage."

That was all Edwyn needed to confirm the reason for Swanson's visit. Seeing Ludnow was clearly sweet on Derryn, he thought it best not to mention she had just lost Powell's child.

24

THE HORRIBLE
REALISATION

Megan Powell summoned Mrs Dutton to the library after lunch. She sat at a small writing desk facing a window overlooking the immaculately manicured formal gardens and the rolling landscape further in the distance. When she saw Mrs Dutton, the lady of the house pulled out a chair for her and indicated that she should sit.

> "This is very difficult for me, Mrs Dutton, and I request your honesty and your silence on the matters that I discuss with you today. I am deeply humiliated by the questions I need to ask you. Still, woman to woman, you may understand my predicament—about one of the maids."

Mrs Dutton was taken aback by her candour and dreaded having to respond. She felt she had a sixth sense about where the conversation was going to go.

"Yes, Mrs Powell. You have my word," she answered.

"I can understand your reticence to become involved in this matter between my husband and I—but we have to trust each other if we want to put an end to the darkness that seems to have descended upon my home."

Mrs Dutton nodded.

"There was a lot I wanted to tell you, Mrs Powell, but I was afraid that you would dismiss me when you learned of what I knew."

"I do understand your fears," Megan consoled. "I have great respect for you, Mrs Dutton. No gossip has returned to me regarding what is happening under my roof, and for that I commend you. I appreciate you personally could not intervene to stop my husband's many fits of abuse of the household staff."

"Do we know the whereabouts of the widow, Mrs Evans? Have you received any information regarding her?"

Mrs Dutton paused and took a deep breath. Sadly, it was not long enough to compose her thoughts and find a gentle way to break the news.

"I heard Mr Powell and Swanson talking a couple of nights ago. Apparently, Mr Powell had instructed Swanson to collect something from Dr Pritchard that was to be administered to Derryn—Mrs Evans."

"Have you any idea what he needed from the doctor?"

"I don't know for sure, Mrs Powell, but I have a theory about what they were up to."

"Speak freely, Mrs Dutton. There is little that can surprise me about my husband anymore."

Mrs Dutton was terrified of what the consequences of her revelation would be. Still, she felt a duty, to tell the truth. There had been too many victims of Ellis Powell's cruelty that Mrs Dutton and seen during her lengthy tenure. *I am the only person who would possibly shed light on the events and stop anyone else from falling victim to Mr Powell's lascivious ways.*

"Swanson returned from the village quite late and went straight to the Master's study. I am ashamed to say this, Mrs Powell, but I eavesdropped on them. This is not usual behaviour for me, I assure you. But their discussion was about the girl, and I was worried about her."

"And the tablets?" asked Megan Powell.

"I believe that the doctor supplied tablets to bring down babies, to abort them."

"Are you sure?"

"Yes. It was on hearing that news I told her Mrs Evans she must flee. Those tablets have a habit of killing the mother as well as the child. I got the impression that would not trouble Mr Powell in the slightest."

Megan looked mortified. *I know Ellis had a roving eye, and more, but forcing women who lived under our roof into 'backstreet' abortions is a new low, even for him.*

"That explains why the girl ran off in the middle of the night, Mrs Dutton, does it not?"

"Yes."

Mrs Dutton looked nervous, not wanting to continue, but Mrs Powell's steely gaze compelled her to reveal everything she knew about that monster of a husband of hers.

"We had a maid here some time ago, Emily Jennings. The young orphan girl you took on to work here."

"Yes, I remember her. Go on."

"Well, she also fell pregnant by the master. She was so beside herself with despair that she told me her monthlies were late. She came back a few days later to tell me that the master had arranged medicine from the doctor that would 'solve the problem.' He— Mr Powell—practically forced the pills down her gullet himself. When she came to, she was instructed to leave and never come back, or Swanson would take her to the hunting lodge and deal with her."

Megan kicked herself for her tardiness. *I should have gone and checked that lodge out as sooner.*

"Have you ever heard from her? Miss Jennings?"

"No, Ma'am."

"There was also another maid, Betty Lumsden, who was promised a great deal of money if she accompanied your husband and Mr Swanson to the hunting lodge on her weekend off. She had a child in Cardiff living with her mother, and they were penniless. She needed every penny that she could earn. I was led to believe the experience was sordid and brutal. Dr Pritchard was there too, as I understand it."

"Doctor Pritchard? Well, I don't know what to make of all this!" murmured the panicked wife.

She knew that her husband was a predator and that his cruel streak stretched into the bedroom, but Dr Pritchard seemed to be a respectable man of the community. She thought back to their wedding night and the utter disaster it had been. Young and inexperienced, his drunken and lustful violence had horrified her. She had run from the bedroom and locked herself in a linen cupboard, silently sobbing until the following morning.

"How did Derryn become entangled in this mess?"

"Derryn, already a young widow, became an alcoholic after the unexpected death of her daughter. She used to go drinking in The Dragon pub in the village. One night when Swanson was drunk, he boasted to the livery boy that he had stood outside the widow's cottage one night, the one she rented the cottage from Dr Pritchard. He said the master had bought her quite a lot of drinks and she was very unsteady on her feet. Mr Powell offered to walk her home, and Swanson secretly followed on behind. When they got to Mrs Evan's cottage, he saw the master go inside and ply her with more drink. The master had suggested to her they should have a nightcap. Then the master had his way with her as she lay on the bed, not moving a muscle, apparently. Out cold, she was. Swanson peeked through the bedroom window and watched everything. The master was delighted, saying that Mrs Evans would be too drunk to remember what he had done, judgin' by the state she was in when he left the cottage."

Mrs Dutton took a deep breath to give her a moment to assess how Mrs Powell was taking the ugly news. Megan was sat stony-faced, staring into the distance. Her sense of duty made Mrs Dutton reluctantly continue with the gamekeeper's account.

"Swanson laughed and told the boy that Mrs Evans craved drink so badly she was prepared to do anything to get it. That the master had the opportunity to do terrible things to her in return for drink. He used to drop off bottles by her bed and an empty wage packet. She was trapped, partly by addiction and partly because she had no money. He knew she could never escape, or so he thought. I warned her to leave before they made her take the tablets. He hatched a plan that she should throw herself on the mercy of one of her old friends in the village until she could get back on her feet again financially."

Megan Powell was visibly shattered, but not from her husband's adultery. Her love for and loyalty to him had died years ago at the birth of their son. The shame that these atrocities had taken place in her home inflicted on female staff she was doing her best to nurture, to give them a reasonable standard of living, cut deep.

"I didn't know. Honestly, I didn't. Not a word reached my ears. Mrs Dutton, please instruct the stables to have my horse ready within an hour."

"Yes, Ma'am," answered Mrs Dutton, sick to her stomach.

The housekeeper didn't know whether the decision to confide in Mrs Powell would result in anything positive. She knew that if Swanson got wind of their conversation—he would kill her.

In his hurry to fetch the doctor, Robbie had not had much time to explain, other than medical help was urgently needed. When he arrived at the farm, Dr Pritchard was visibly shaken at the sight of Swanson with his throat ripped out, lying awkwardly in a pool of blood on the kitchen floor.

"There's not a lot I can do for this poor fellow!" exclaimed the doctor.

"No, Doc. We need help with a young woman. She's upstairs! Quick!"

When he saw Derryn lying on the bed, Dr Pritchard flinched, realising that he would have to navigate this event very carefully to avoid slipping into a precarious position. If he was linked to Swanson and Powell and their hunting lodge activities, he could be convicted and sent to jail or have his license revoked. No licence to practice would reduce him to be an illegal back-alley abortionist or sewing up gangsters who were trying to escape the law.

It would be easy to kill Derryn. The nick of an artery was all it took. She harboured a tremendous amount of information that could incriminate him—and Ellis. Still, he didn't dare have this patient die. There were too many people watching.

He lifted up the covers and removed the nightshirt from between her legs. He saw the congealing blood and tissue and instantly knew the cause. *I am surprised that Ellis Powell had not asked for the usual remedy to the problem. Why did he resort to this rash approach, the fool?*

He deduced that Derryn was unconscious from loss of blood, and needed to make sure she didn't lose anymore, else it would have been the end of her.

"She has miscarried. I need to examine her," the doctor advised. "Please wait outside."

Ludnow hadn't spoken a word till this moment.

"I am going nowhere," he growled.

"Usually, men don't attend these procedures."

"I assure you, there is nothing usual about this situation, Dr Pritchard."

"I will refuse to treat h—"

Ludnow felt a surge of wrath rise from deep within his being.

"—You will not leave this room alive if you kill her. I will break your neck with my bare hands. Now set to work, man."

The doctor knew there was a certain kind of man it was best not to argue with—the placid kind who were moved to fury by someone threatening their loved ones. The doctor had seen enough bedside vigils to sense that Ludnow was one of those men. With reluctance, he set to work saving the woman's life, rolling up his sleeves and starting the procedure. All the while, Ludnow sat on a chair next to the bed, watching every move that Pritchard made. Keen to make it look like he had done everything he could, he stayed two hours to observe his patient, taking her pulse at her limp wrist, and pulling her eyelids up to see if her pupils responded. In time, the doctor was relieved she seemed to be strengthening. *Damn you, Swanson, for resorting to your fists, you crass oaf.*

Afterwards, as Pritchard cleaned his hands, panic began to rise up again. From the moment he saw the gamekeeper lying on the floor dead, he knew that the game was up for him too. There would be no time to sell his house or practice. *My only option is to flee the area. Take the train to the city and never return. Take a ship to a distant land. But I'll always be looking over my shoulder. Be a fugitive for the rest of my life. Why did I ever let Ellis Powell talk me into being so complicit in his depraved desires?*

A determined Megan Powell raided the stables for warm clothes, covering herself from head-to-toe with oilskins and a thick felt hat. She left Rodyr Hall and rode into the bleak countryside with purpose and determination, having heard about the hunting lodge, but never yet visiting the place. By the sound of it, it didn't seem to have an ambience that she would enjoy.

Swanson had revelled in describing the horror of the place at length, hoping that it would dissuade her from visiting unexpectedly. His plan worked. He eulogised about the stuffed animals that adorned the sideboards and windowsills. The floor was covered with hides. The walls were festooned with grizzly trophies. He said the dead glass eyes seemed to watch wherever you moved. Shotguns lined the walls and hunting knives littered the tables. For Swanson, it was a shrine to brutal violence. For Megan, it sounded like the embodiment of hell itself.

The hunting lodge was a fair distance from the hall. It was madness to attempt the ride this late in the afternoon, the light fading by the minute as the winter sunset early. The horses' hooves crunched through the frosty fields. It was a reliable animal, but she had never ridden him at night. She had the foresight to put an oil lamp in her saddlebag. To sustain her along the journey, Mrs Dutton had supplied a few rounds of thick cheese and ham sandwiches with extra butter.

Megan Powell had travelled three and a half miles before she saw the lights of the lodge come into view. The lodge was set on a rocky outcrop which served as a lookout over the wild woodland below. The range flora and fauna in the area was both abundant and magnificent. *Why is it men cannot resist killing to quench their bloodlust?* In a reflective mood, she slowed down. As the horse trotted toward the lodge, she wondered how she would deal with her monstrous husband.

Hearing the clip-clop of hooves, Ellis looked out of the window and the rider approaching. He stepped out onto the path and shouted:

"Where on earth have you been, Swanson? I am waiting for news. Hurry up, man!"

When the horse got closer, he realised that it wasn't Swanson. *Perhaps its Pritchard?* When the rider dismounted and strode towards him, finally, he recognised the figure. *Megan!*

"What a lovely surprise!" Ellis called to her, in an attempt to sound natural. "I am delighted to see you, darling. You must be freezing. Let me show you around. How about a nice cup of tea to warm you up?"

"No, thank you," was his wife's terse reply.

As she got closer, he tried to kiss her cheek. In no mood for his romantic manoeuvre, she dodged it and went straight into the lodge. For Megan, the warmth of the golden fire was lost on her. The cold, grim hunting trophies staring down at her blackened her mood further.

"I was expecting, Swanson," Ellis said cheerily.

"Yes, I heard you before."

Her husband looked worried. *What if—*

"What news are you waiting for, Ellis?"

"Oh, just some business that I am doing. I asked Swanson to collect a note from the postman. If you don't want tea, a whisky, perhaps?"

She thought of Derryn and his exploitation of her weakness. She owed it to the woman to refuse.

"No, thank you. I shan't be here long."

"You surely don't intend to go back in the dark, Megan. It's too dangerous, my love."

"I shall do as I please. Do not lecture me."

From that response, Ellis knew that this was no friendly visit.

"The maid, Derryn Evans, the young widow from the village—" She made sure he knew exactly who she was speaking about. "Well, she is still missing, and nobody can find her."

Ellis was instantly filled with fury for his wife. *How dare she question me, challenge me?* However, given that her father bankrolled their household and their comfortable lifestyle, he was not in a position to fight back.

"She is likely holed up somewhere. I sent Swanson to look for her at Ludnow Gravis' farm. I told him to bring her here if he found her."

He had blurted out the reply without thinking. It was a significant error on his part.

"Bring her here to the lodge, Ellis? Why?"

"Forget about it. I meant the 'hall' not 'here'. The woman needs a good talking to and to buck her ideas up. She cannot walk away from her duties whenever the fancy takes her. Mrs Dutton needs to bring her into line if you ask me—"

"Let us get down to business, Ellis. The situation between us cannot continue as it is," she replied.

For a moment there was a ray of light in Ellis' unsure future. *I bet she wants a divorce. If I negotiate a reasonable settlement, then life won't be too bad.* However, as quickly as he had become hopeful, those hopes were dashed.

"I know about your affairs with the staff, Ellis, and I know how you terminate the pregnancies with the doctor's help."

Ellis desperately needed Swanson to arrive. He formulated a plan to eliminate Megan. He had the perfect cover story. *She is recklessly riding into the darkness on uncertain ground. The horse will throw her. She falls and breaks her neck. I inherit the hall, and my secrets are safe.* However, Swanson had not arrived, and Ellis was becoming more agitated.

"You have tortured women for years, and I am not tolerating a monster like you under my roof any longer."

Ellis could no longer contain his anger.

"How dare you refer to me as a monster you cold-hearted, frigid harpy? You lock yourself in that bedroom every night, and I can't come near you. What did you expect me to do? You always remind me it is 'your house', not 'ours' thanks to your family fortune. Do you know how sick I am of our arrangement? I am the master of that hall, not you. Do you hear me? I should have beaten sense into you until you submitted to me. Just like I did with the servants. Just like I did with the harlots Swanson brought here for me. Your decision to leave our bed is the cause of my behaviour. Your failure to be a good wife makes you responsible for the pregnancies, the abortions, and the deaths."

Megan fought to keep the fear from her voice, her earlier bravado evaporating.

"Deaths? What deaths Ellis?"

Ellis felt had nothing to lose, now beyond fury. He'd already decided he was going to kill her as she was preparing to leave. He would apply one blow to the back of her head after which he would hook her foot in the horse's stirrup. Then would use the crop on the animal, and it would bolt in fear and take flight into the fields. The horse would drag Megan along the ground, and there would be nothing left of her when she was found. It was the perfect murder.

The plan soothed him, and he gained confidence, he calmed down and spoke to her in a normal tone.

> "Swanson and I have a lot of fun here, my dear—all the fun that you refuse to give me. Of course, we have had ladies like you who refuse to play along. They can be persuaded. Although, we don't dare let them go, afterwards so we play with them a little while and when we have had our fill, well—" He pointed to the hunting knives. "—Swanson takes care of them."

> "How?" asked a sickened and fearful Megan.

> "Come with me, my darling. Let me show you how ingenious Swanson is."

He opened the door of the Lodge and stepped outside, but his wife was rooted to the spot still. He walked back to her and roughly, he took her gloved hand, then frogmarched her to the cliff edge. Feeling her tremble uncontrollably made him feel calmer about what was to come.

They reached the edge of the cliff, and Ellis put his hands into his coat pockets, surveying the wildland below him.

> "Look at that countryside," he revelled. "Wild and free, isn't it?"

He walked closer to the edge, then peered down.

"There are so many predators in that wilderness. Cats and foxes. A body cannot remain intact for long."

"You threw them off the cliff?"

"Not me, Swanson. Remember." he snarled. "Well, some we allowed to get away, they literally ran across these fields naked to escape us." Ellis guffawed. "I would say Swanson disposed of about five girls, mostly prostitutes we lured from the cities. No one ever missed women like them."

The enormity of the crime was all too much for Megan.

"And Dr Pritchard? He was aware of all this?"

"Of course, my dear," Ellis smiled, beginning to enjoy the conversation, delighting in twisting a verbal knife into his loveless spouse. "As a matter of fact, Pritchard was a very helpful chap—performed quite a few operations for us. He would come up here once a month, too, for a little treat. So, you know, he liked being paid in kind just as much as with money. From his point of view, a single man like him, it was very worthwhile."

He turned his back to the cliff and looked at her. Sensing she was in deep trouble, Megan knew she had to use the one powerful weapon she had left. Her body. She stared deeply into his eyes and did her best to feign love and compassion. She put up her hand to stroke his cheek.

"Oh, Ellis, you are right! I can see it now. I haven't met your needs as a wife. I must try to learn to satisfy you," she sighed, and gave a little smile.

Ellis interpreted it as a reprieve, the entire conversation had taken on a repentant quality. His mind was reeling with euphoria. He had convinced her. He had converted her. *And if she falls out of line again, it will be effortless to frighten her into submission.*

"Megan, do you still have feelings for me? Will you ever give me up to the authorities?"

Ellis' ego was getting the better of him, he wanted absolute power, he wanted total commitment, and he was begging for an answer. She moved toward him slowly, her face now inches from his, and she stared up at him sympathetically.

"Of course, not Ellis," she said tenderly. "I will never have my son's future ruined. I will never have my son watch his father hang."

Ellis was overwhelmed by her commitment and forgiveness. At last, after all these years, she seemed to be behaving like a supportive wife should.

But Megan was not committed, and she was not forgiving. She was sickened and disgusted. Taking a step back from him to give herself some space, the humiliated wife stretched out her arms in front of her as if planning to embrace him. Then, she lunged forward, putting her full body weight behind the attack, propelling herself forward forcefully. Her outstretched hands hit Ellis in the chest like a sledgehammer, causing him to topple. He staggered backwards until only one of his feet found solid ground. The other foot dangled in the air with nothing underneath it. It felt like time itself had slowed. Ellis teetered on the precipice, his arms flailing, fingers grasping at thin air. It was not enough to regain his balance. He regretted wasting time reprimanding his wife when he should have been staging her murder. His ego had cost him his life. He went sailing backwards off the cliff, screaming for mercy as he finally overbalanced. The screams receded as he fell further and further then abruptly stopped.

The beleaguered wife smiled. *Ellis Powell will never trouble me again. Nor will he ever harm another woman. Nor taint his young son. I hope the foxes are hungry tonight.*

Later that evening, finally, after a slow and sure-footed ride, Megan returned to Rodyr Hall. The staff were huddled around the great kitchen table, unusual because it was way past dinner. It was a sign they were anxious for her to return. As the kitchen door open, everybody stood up out of respect. She nodded for them to sit down.

Mrs Dutton remained standing. Megan could see that the housekeeper was concerned.

"Is everything in order, Mrs Dutton?" asked Megan, keen to put on a front that everything was alright.

Mrs Dutton cleared her throat.

"No, Ma'am," she answered nervously. "We have a situation, and we don't know how to deal with it."

"Well, what has happened?"

"We have been waiting for you to get home," continued Mrs Dutton.

Megan nodded her head impatiently, not wanting to say anything until she had a plan for explaining Elli's disappearance.

"Well, Ludnow Gravis and the two farm boys delivered the body of Mr Swanson here just after you left. He is stone dead."

The mistress of the house was not interested in the details.

"So, where is he now?" she asked impatiently.

"We have him in the short tunnel leading into the icehouse. What do you want us to do with him? He needs to be buried as soon as possible—his throat was ripped out by a dog."

"Swanson will not be buried on my land. I do not want him anywhere near me. Put him on the wagon in the morning and deliver him to Reverend Hughes. He can do whatever he likes with him. I don't care."

Mrs Powell thought that whatever message Ludnow Gravis was sending her husband, it was too late. The Lord of the Manor was not there to receive it.

25

THE CALLING

Everyone had rushed into action at Ludnow's farm. George and Edwyn helped Ludnow take care of Swanson's remains. The two Baker boys scrubbed down the kitchen and the stairs. Francis and Bronwyn took care of Derryn. It was bedlam. When they all eventually left, Ludnow breathed a sigh of relief. Well-meaning though they were, he wasn't comfortable with people near him. He had lived a solitary life for over ten years, and he was happy that way.

He put the kettle on the stove and went about brewing some tea. He took a cup up to Derryn who was still settled in his bed. She was awake, but she looked weak. Her eyes were dull, and she lacked energy. Still, she had lost the ghostly grey pallor that he had seen earlier in the day. As she sipped at the hot, sweet liquid, Ludnow knew she would need more than that to sustain her as she recovered from the miscarriage. He disappeared downstairs, then reappeared with another tray of refreshments. He took the small bowl of stew and fed it to her as if she were a small child. Feeling queasy, she didn't want to eat and would shake her head, making things difficult for Ludnow. However, he would coax her, telling her to take some deep breaths, and then delivered another spoonful.

"Do you feel better now?"

"Yes, thank you."

He went to leave, thinking she would benefit from the rest, but she reached out and put her hand over his, pushing it down into the eiderdown.

"Don't go. Please? Stay with me. I don't want to be alone."

It was more than ten years since a woman had touched him with such kindness, and he didn't know what to do. Self-consciously, he pulled his hand away and covered her up. For the need of a distraction, he picked up the supper tray and turned to leave the bedroom.

"Are you coming back?" she called to him.

He looked at her and nodded.

"I am afraid," she confessed.

"I know. I won't leave you on your own."

Derryn heard him downstairs as he tidied up after the meal. Exhausted, her eyes soon closed.

Ludnow woke up first and felt a woman's body next to his. In her sleep, she had thrown her arm across his chest. He heard John and Robbie arriving and the dogs scratching to get outside, but he didn't move. He had fallen asleep next to her still in the clothes he had worn the day before.

Gravis had denied himself human contact for such a long time that he couldn't take the risk of moving lest she woke up and pulled her arm away. He lay like that for a long time, absorbing the warmth that she radiated. Eventually, to Ludnow's disappointment, the spell was broken as she opened her eyes. He was sure she would move away.

"Good morning," she whispered.

"Hello," he replied, suppressing the urge to kiss her on her forehead.

"Did you sleep well?" she asked.

"The best I have in years. Are you hungry?"

Feeling awkward, thrown by the strength of his emotions, he made a move to return to the kitchen.

"No, don't go yet," she begged. "Stay a little longer."

Ludnow laughed at her.

"You would make an appalling farmer's wife! You can't shy away from early starts."

"How long have you lived here?" asked Derryn, realising she still knew very little about the man next to her.

"Most of my life," he replied.

"Really? I hope you don't mind me asking, but the villagers see you as a stranger?"

"Yes. I inherited it from my parents. But there was a time when I lived somewhere else."

"I have to explain a lot of things to you," she said.

Second-guessing her burden, he took the sting from her confession.

"You don't have to explain anything to me. I know your struggle with liquor if that's what you're referring to?"

"Oh," she said, feeling ashamed. Everybody in the village must have known.

"I found you on the side of the road one night and took you back home to your cottage."

She had a sudden flashback to that night when she felt safe in the arms of the stranger. For her, the sense of connection between them deepened.

"Was that y—"

Ludnow cut her short.

"That was the past, Derryn. You had terrible hardships to deal with. Now, you must look to the future."

"But, the miscarriage? I thought you would at least want to know who the f—"

She couldn't complete the sentence.

"Derryn, whatever has happened to you before you walked into this farmhouse is none of my business, and I will never hold your past against you."

"Then at least you will let me ask something about your background?"

He nodded.

"Why—" she hesitated. "Why did you become the sin-eater?"

This would be the first time Ludnow explained to anyone what had led him to choose such a polarising role in the community.

"I was raised in this valley," began Ludnow. "My parents weren't poor, but they were of limited means. In those days, it was much harder on the farmers. Today, we have tools and machines to help us, but in those days, my father did everything alone. My mother was a pillar of strength, and she fought tooth and nail to educate us."

"Us?" asked Derryn.

"Yes. I have three brothers and a sister."

"Do they love you?"

The question took him off guard, and he paused.

"Yes, they do, I suppose. In their own way, but I have stayed away from them for a long time. I won a scholarship to a university and chose to do engineering. Those were good years," he said with a hint of a smile. "I had a passion for shipbuilding," he continued, "and I found a job at the Belfast shipyards. I also found a girl while I was there. Her name was Anna, and I fell in love with her. We got married soon after and had a little boy."

Ludnow was finding it difficult to speak, he had not talked about his family for many years, and he was engulfed by emotion. Derryn moved closer to him and lay her head on his chest. She thought it might be easier for him if he didn't have to hold eye contact.

"His name was Thomas, like my father, and he was a joy," Ludnow said fondly. "He had brown hair and blue eyes like me. And he was charming and clever. But he only lived until he was four years old."

Ludnow paused.

"Our shipbuilding company had been given a contract to construct one of the largest ships in the world, so on the night we completed it, instead of going home like I usually did, I went to the pub to have a few rounds with my colleagues. One became two, and two became three."

"Is this why you never drink?" asked Derryn.

Ludnow nodded.

"I left the pub very late, and when I got into my street, it was chaos. There were policeman and fire carts and neighbours filling the street."

He took a deep breath, his voice beginning to crack under the strain of retelling the tale.

"I realised that they were all standing in front of my house. It had caught on fire."

Derryn gasped.

"Neither Anna nor Thomas survived—the blaze took them both."

"Oh, no!" she said quietly.

She could feel his stubbly chin brushing against her forehead, and his hot, damp teardrops soaking into her hair.

"I watched my wife be buried and also had to watch the little white coffin sink into the ground."

Derryn could see Becca's coffin as if it were yesterday. Her empathy for him filled her with deep sorrow. She was heartbroken at the memory of her loss, and for Ludnow's as well.

"If I had been at home, it would never have happened. I would have saved them. I know I would. I was ravaged by guilt. I couldn't stay in Belfast, and so I came back here. Through Efa, I began to rebuild myself, atone, by consuming the sins of others. Every time that I did it, I felt that I was saving a soul, even if mine was doomed to hell. I believe that God reads our motives in a different way to men."

"I hope so."

Then Derryn became very fierce.

"When we are married, you will never perform that ritual again. Do you hear me, Ludnow?"

He smiled. She was already telling him what to do.

"Is that a proposal, Derryn Evans?"

"I believe it is. There has been too much sadness here. Too many bad memories. Let's leave this God-forsaken village and make a new life for ourselves."

"Where? Cardiff?" he laughed.

"I think we can be more adventurous than that! Let's take a steamship to America!"

26

EPILOGUE

The Montana sky stretched from horizon to horizon, and the green grass stopped at the base of the mountains. The white-hot sun sat high up in the air and shone its glorious light and heat upon the ground. A pale clapboard house stood in the centre of a field of crops.

There were wooden chairs on the veranda overlooking the pretty flowers in the garden. The barn next to the farmhouse was painted bright red, decorated with windows frames that were pure white. The house was cheerful inside with bright coloured curtains and coverings, patterned crockery hung in the dressers, and the walls were filled with art.

Ludnow and Derryn lay in their bedroom, lapping up the peace of a warm summer's morning. Ludnow rolled over and looked at her. She was his pride and joy. His everything. Her face had filled out, and the sun had added a rosy glow to her cheeks. Her body had curves, her breasts were full, and she had regained her voluptuous figure of days gone by. He kissed her on her forehead and brushed her hair out of her face with his hand.

The dark shadows of their past were behind them now. They had undoubtedly taken the scenic route through life. The only compensation for their tragedy was that they had found each other.

He went to lie on top of her. As he moved, she said with a smile:

"One of these days my belly will be too big to do this."

"Oh my! When will the bairn be due?"

"In the spring."

"But how?"

"Now, that's a silly question. Surely you know by now?" chuckled Derryn.

He kissed her face, and then her mouth, his passion rising.

"I love you, Derryn," whispered Ludnow Gravis, the man of few words.

"I know," she replied, "I love you too."

***

For another rural Victorian village saga check out the next book in the series:

The Urchin of Walton Hall

Aged just ten, love-child Bess is abandoned at Walton Hall by her desperate and sickly mother.

She is promptly sent away by her philandering father, the colliery owner Robert Harvey, to become an educated and accomplished young woman. It has one other advantage, it allows her to escape the beatings at the cruel hand of her vengeful stepmother, Hannah.

As Bess finishes boarding school, a tragic accident strikes her father. The decline of the family's fortunes means Bess and her siblings must find spouses to provide for them.

After a series of doomed arranged encounters with potential suitors, Bess's stepmother takes drastic action against her to protect herself and her family.

Who is the mystery fiancé Hannah Harvey has in mind?

And how will Bess feel knowing the decision means she will never be free to marry her childhood sweetheart?

Buy The Urchin of Walton Hall or view all of my books on Amazon.

***

Can you help this book reach more people?

Please consider leaving an honest review on Amazon so more readers can enjoy the story.

***

Join me on Facebook for more Victorian snippets and to find out what I am working on next. Thank you so much for your support. It means everything.

Best wishes,

Emma

Printed in Great Britain
by Amazon